IT HAD TO BE YOU

IT HAD TO BE YOU

The Joan and Ernest Story

Melissa Malouf

iUniverse, Inc.
New York Lincoln Shanghai

It Had to Be You
The Joan and Ernest Story

All Rights Reserved © 1997, 2004 by Melissa Malouf

No part of this book may be reproduced or transmitted in any form or by any means, graphic, electronic, or mechanical, including photocopying, recording, taping, or by any information storage retrieval system, without the written permission of the publisher.

iUniverse, Inc.

For information address:
iUniverse, Inc.
2021 Pine Lake Road, Suite 100
Lincoln, NE 68512
www.iuniverse.com

Second edition

This is a work of fiction. All characters and events represented herein are imagined, and any resemblance to actual people or events, living or dead, is coincidental.

ISBN: 0-595-32324-3

Printed in the United States of America

*For my parents,
Glenn and Marla,
who gave me the music.*

*Some others I've seen
Might never be mean,
Might never be cross
Or try to be boss,
But they wouldn't do...*

—Gus Kahn

Contents

Speak Low 2
Dancing in the Dark 10
Love and Marriage 19
Me and My Gal 32
Someone to Watch over Me 42
Pillow Talk 50
I've Got You under My Skin 61
I'm in the Mood for Love 75
It Had to Be You 88
Where or When 97
What'll I Do? 107
But Not for Me 117
About the Author 129

* * *

Young Ernest had of course been warned, and more than once, never to talk to strangers. But who could have been more strange—the smell of her, the lacey hem of her slip, the breasts as stiff as party hats, pressing beneath her white blouse—than the very person who issued the warning as she sent him outside to play? So that, in heeding the warning, he rarely spoke to anyone, as little as possible to his mysterious mother, certainly not to the stroller-pushing passersby who wore the same white blouses and who sometimes greeted him, "Hey there, little fella," as he sat in the front yard playing the quiet game of pretending to be someone else. Nor did he speak to the all-by-herself lady across the street who made donuts every Saturday for the neighborhood children, from whom he would accept a donut with the fearful solemnity of a secret doubter who nevertheless receives the communion wafer.

Once he went too far, wandered off his street to the next block, which looked just the same as his own, same small stucco houses, same squared-off patches of front yard, same palm trees and poisonous oleanders, same strangers lifting grocery bags from cars, lifting babies, carrying the bags and the babies into dark garages where there would be a door to the kitchen. What wasn't the same was the old man watering his lawn, a man outside during the day and it wasn't a Saturday or a Sunday. This had never happened on his own block, this was new, a new kind of stranger that the boy could not help staring at. He stood at the edge of the man's green lawn, smelling sweet cigar smoke, drawn without knowing that he was drawn by the reds and blues of the man's plaid shirt, and he utterly forgot his mother's warning when the man approached and asked, "Where do you live, boy?" He answered, pointing, "Right here," thinking that he was pointing over there, up the street, toward the other block of houses. But within the awkwardness of having spoken, of hearing his own voice, he pointed more at himself than at anything else. And so he thought the old man must have been pretending when he said, "Me too, boy. Me too."

* * *

Speak Low

Ernest's father told him as they sat on stools not too close together in an out-of-the-way bar that the one thing he would never do to a woman is shoot her.

Ernest let this remark hang there between them for a while. Long enough for it to take on the shape of the woman who used to get home from the movies in time to make dinner for her silent son. The woman who used to turn on the radio, tape her latest academy award predictions onto the refrigerator, laugh at something the radio said, and always look at young Ernest as if he were a curiosity, something with amusing appendages that she could see but he couldn't.

And now it dawned on him why his father had put him off all these months, why he had sent a brief note reporting that he'd had "a surgery," but that Ernest was to stay put in Cambridge and study his "goddamned geology," that he was not to fly out to Los Angeles until further notice. His father had put him off so that neither of them would feel ashamed. So that he could buy some time, learn to speak all over again. So that the removal of his larynx would not prevent him from telling his son that the one thing he would never do to a woman is shoot her.

"Are we talking about my mother?"

"No."

"She's not who you're referring to?"

"No. All of them."

"I don't like this."

"What don't you like?"

"I can't tell if you're kidding."

"Too bad."

"What are you saying, Dad?"

"You have to look at me. Watch my mouth."

"I know."
"And con-cen-trate."
"It's not the words. I can follow you. It's what you mean."
"You're not list-en-ing."

Ernest remembered his father's voice, though he had not heard it often, his father all those years at work too early or too late, Ernest learning as a child that inside the house his mother's radio did all the talking. So that after he had left for college, then graduate school, after his mother had boarded an apparently perennial tour bus, and his father kept in touch only through thorny telegraphic notes, it was not easy for Ernest to recall the miracle of those occasional Sunday afternoons outside in the yard: father and son among the yellowing tomato plants, young Ernest digging in the sandy dirt when out of nowhere he would hear his father's voice begin to speak, to tell its own story of the velvet voice that got me the job, are you listening, kid? got me the job in a Hollywood studio within a week, *one week*, everyone in their cold apartments eating potatoes back in Philadelphia, P.A. telling me I'm crazy to go to California where there's nothing but movie stars that don't give the time of day to the man on the street and no churches next door where a kid like you who never lets his father know what he's thinking can get some sense knocked into him. They called me a lunatic, that whole branch of the family that never moves except to shake their heads back and forth. *California!* Back and forth. But what did they say when I got a job in one week in a Hollywood studio where my voice made people call each other over to hear and a va-va-voom woman in a blue dress said my voice was like a velvet glove, and where the man in charge said I would be the general assistant and nobody, not *nobody* gives me disrespect. They didn't even send me packing when everything crashed, gave me—this is the kind of people I'm talking about—gave me a twenty dollar bonus when my son, meaning you, is born in '30, a bonus in that day and age. And what do you think the relatives back in Philly said when I had a wife in two months, that's all it took. After a movie I'd take her for coffee and she'd say, Say something, Jerry. Say a hard word. So I'd lean across the table and say *pharmaceutical* or *Czechoslovakia*, and I'm telling you, kid, the blood would go like a splash across your mother's face no matter what word I picked. What a girl she was then! I sent them a photograph, me and my blond wife standing in front of the palm trees next to the house, everything getting paid for fair and square, and what do you think they said when they saw all this? They said nothing, what else?

Ernest's father signaled the bartender for another round. "If you keep them out, they take re-venge," he told his son.

"They take what?"

"Re-venge."

"Don't talk too fast."

"I know."

"You mean they leave. The way my mother did."

"No. I mean they stay. To see how far you will go. If you will pull the trigger."

"I get it."

"You don't get an-y-thing."

"I don't have a gun."

"You don't have a wo-man."

"You don't either, Dad."

They looked away from each other and watched the bartender, a Brooklyn Dodgers fan, pick up the radio with both hands, hold it as if it were a watermelon, and talk into the ragged net that covered the small speaker. "This is it," he was saying. "This is the year. I've been telling you guys all along and for once you better listen to me."

"Mother left," Ernest continued. "So we're not talking about her."

"I said that. Are you deaf?"

"What about afterwards. The women. You had some good times."

"And be-fore."

"You want me to be surprised, but I'm not."

"Yes you are."

"You had your own life. We all did."

"I still do."

"I know."

"You don't know."

"I picked you up, Dad. Remember? I saw him."

"My room-mate. Char-lie."

"It doesn't matter."

"I can do what-ev-er I want. Out in the o-pen."

"The perfect marriage."

Ernest looked at his white-haired father, at the box of batteries tucked into his shirt pocket like a pack of cigarettes, at the wire that connected the batteries to the plastic pipe-like device he put into his mouth in order to speak, at the gauzy scarf that protected the hole in his throat, and at the way his father managed these props with professional aplomb, disguising the effort, as if the operation had turned him into David Niven.

Which is what made Ernest remember the evening when his father got home from work early for a change, and it was going to be just the two of them, and they were going to eat beans and franks and potato chips for dinner while his mother went to the movies with the next-door neighbor, a dark-haired divorcée whom the adolescent Ernest dreamed about half awake, half afraid the dream might come true, there was so much of her. He was wondering if his father dreamed about her too as he saw the door close behind the swirl of his mother's flowery skirt and then heard his father's voice erupt, What are you? twelve now? seems to me the time has come, a boy your age can know a father's secret. That's how old I was when your grandfather let me in on his, took me down to the basement where your grandmother never allowed me to go because she was afraid of it, and I believed her until the night he took me down there, one light bulb hanging over the table he'd set up, and all over this table were his notebooks, the kind with bindings that look like real books, you know the kind. But what you don't know is that inside these notebooks was his collection of flowers, grasses, leaves, every damn thing like that he could find was glued on each page, one by one, as neat and scientific as could be. You couldn't tell there was glue with the naked eye—you know that expression? the naked eye? no magnifying glass, no nothing—to the naked eye it was like the stuff just grew there on the pages, fresh as a morning, and on every page he'd written out the fancy name of each specimen in printing like you never saw in your life. With those ugly butcher's hands of his he'd copied the names out of books from the library, said he couldn't understand the Latin but liked the way it looked, which knowing you, you'd like it too, but it's something you'll never see. He threw it all in the furnace before he died, and I'm sorry now he did, but I'll tell you something, when he first showed me, I thought it was the sissiest secret I ever heard of. Are you listening, kid?

Ernest had been listening and thinking about how he would like to keep the dark-haired divorcée in a secret place in the basement that he'd fix up, nice, with a jewelry box and a French perfume atomizer, and he was wondering if he would ever show her to anybody when he heard his father start to sing in that melt-in-your-mouth voice, better than any voice on the radio, an effortless creamy sound so full of kept promises and easy answers that Ernest squirmed, giggled almost, tried to resist the spell of that voice set to music because it made him love his father too much—that hollow-cheeked lightweight man who had begun to dance to his own velvety music, who was gesturing for his son to join him. Which Ernest finally did, shy at first, and clumsy, but adept enough at learning the words and imitating his father's playful wistful two-step through the lyrics that he was soon within the power of his father's secret, singing in his in-between voice as if he were not himself, as if his body were meant to be seen, as if he were debonair, carefree, as if the divorcée were in the audience, chest heaving. *Somethin's gotta give, somethin's gotta give, somethin's gotta give.*

"Your roommate is none of my business," said Ernest.
"He used to play pi-a-no at the Roos-e-velt Ho-tel."
"I'm not asking you to tell me about him."
"Speak low. When you speak love. His rule of thumb."
"It's none of my business, Dad."
"You stu-dy hell, but you are not so smart as you think."
"Are you trying to give me advice? Is that what this is all about?"
"Yes."

Ernest has not forgotten that the two women who were supposed to have been at the movies had walked in on them, had stood side by side at the open front door, the divorcée clapping her gloved hands, bracelets clinking like ice cubes, Ernest's mother saying, Do it again, do it for *us*, both of them wearing smiles that said this was not only better than waiting in a too-long line at the movies, this was better than the movies because they were not supposed to see it. This was private, what was going on between the awkward-age boy and the thinning man and the versions of romance each one had been giving himself over to, twenty maybe thirty minutes of utter self-forgetting—just singing your guts out for women in bare-shouldered evening gowns who would do whatever you wanted and who would whisper things in your ear that would make your mouth water and who would help you build up the courage it took to look in the mirror. And who would never smile that way at your adolescent erection, the way those two did while they stood at the front door, their smiles saying, You can't fool us, we know your thoughts, we don't even have to ask, that's how smart we are. They were so smart that the power of their smartness snuffed out the power of the secret without a struggle, jolted Ernest back into his twelve-year-old body, a numb and humiliated thing unable to hear his father speak the smallest small-talk as he pushed the coffee table back into its place and turned on the radio, unable to eat the beans and franks his father later brought to his room, unable to draw his father aside and make a pact, cross your heart and hope to die, never to do that again, never ever reveal a secret if there was the slightest chance that a woman would get a hold of it.

"Okay. I'll take your advice. I won't shoot anybody. I promise."
"You will want to take fa-tal shots."
"I'm not you, Dad."
"Here. Try this."

Ernest's father was wiping off the pipe, handing it to his son, gesturing for him to put the thing in his mouth and say something, the thin wire stretched to its limit between them.

Ernest went along with it, spoke into the device, said again, "I won't shoot an-y-bo-dy. I pro-mise," tasting plastic and gin and something else he couldn't name, but his father could have. And what Ernest heard let him know that his father could also have told him that the mechanism has a kind of voice of its own, one not geared to mediate any distinctions between fathers and sons, mothers and roommates, reduces them all to a gravelly robotic sameness. So that in sounding out the words Ernest couldn't help but get the joke that had been played on him. He watched his father lean back in a fit of silent laughter—legs kicking with pleasure, fists pedaling the air—and imagined the roar he would have made.

Ernest handed back the pipe. "You got me," he said.
"In-deed."
They finished off their drinks and ordered another round.
"I have some ge-o-lo-gy for you."
"I don't want to hear it, Dad."
"Yes you do."
"Go to hell."
"You have to look at me."
"I am."
"O-kay. You are a rock. There is a lake, near-by. You are picked up. Thrown to the o-ther side of the lake. Which is too far a-way. In mid-air you are gi-ven a mind. You are a-ware of your-self. But you are still a rock. What do you do?"
"I drop. I sink."
"That's right, son."

* * *

From the time that Joan was in grade school, memorizing useful Latin phrases for the nuns at Marymount, she preferred the company of the grown-ups—the glamorous friends of her parents who came to the house for cocktail parties, for Sunday dinner, for brunches and barbecues, for an evening, once, of home movies, during which she moved among them with a tray of canapés, careful that her puffy-sleeved pig-tailed shadow did not appear on the screen and obstruct their view of themselves on vacation, at costume balls, at the country club swimming pool, always laughing, as if being a grown-up were endlessly funny and fun, not at all like being a child.

She liked most of all a man who worked with her father at the hospital and who always came to the house by himself—a small man, as small as a boy of ten or twelve, and shy among the grown-ups. She liked his bushy black eyebrows that went this way and that, vying for attention with the war scar that rose upward from one corner of his mouth like an exclamation point or a question mark, depending on his expression. And she liked the thick white sweaters he always wore, which he told her were made in a foreign land by beautiful maidens who sang all day and most of the night for the men they had lost to the sea. And there were the tricks he performed with his small magical hands just for her, for his "princess"—the nickel appearing from behind her ear, or displayed in his palm one minute and then gone, just like that!

One night he produced for her a phrase they did not teach at school, *omnia vincit amor*. He played the wizard, pulled the words one by one out of the air above her head, then handed them to her, an invisible important secret, a posy of words that she accepted with a solemn bow, all grace and enchantment. But when she repeated the secret in a whisper full of belief, worthy of any sorcerer's apprentice, so that the words seemed to her not only true but alive—she saw the fearless expressions on their fairy-godmother faces—he had laughed, like one of the grown-ups, as if her incantation were one of the oldest jokes in the world. And she was frightened, for even though he was laughing she could see in the small man's sorry eyes that something was worse than wrong. His scar looked like nothing but a scar, and his magical hands lay limp and empty in his lap.

*   *   *

Dancing in the Dark

You would introduce yourself as Joan, and leave it at that. That is, if you were to go out this evening, to some new place, and need to say a name, extend a hand. You would ignore the tremble there, in your hand, if such introductions were in order, if you were not in fact going to stay put, on this New Year's Eve, drinking another vodka gimlet, adding Nick's name to the list of your dead.

Others have longer lists than yours. Genuine tragedies. One must keep things in perspective. Remember that.

And imagine that you are doing something else, that there is no newspaper on the floor in front of your chair, with its brief account of his death, its photograph of the body. Suppose the apartment were filled with partygoers, fellow graduate students, good revelers all, and a flirtatious professor of economics or two, congenital laughers, almost adequate distractions from the story in the newspaper, from the picture on the mantle of your dead parents, from the dying with which you've grown accustomed to living.

If one can call it that, if one can call living this sitting in the dark, this consideration of lists, this setting the record straight. To wit: In two hours and twenty minutes, it will be the first day of a new decade. Nineteen-sixty. Joan is twenty-four years old. Her hair is short and blond, but not impish. Her eyes are blue-gray, but not oceanic. She has not been touched since the last time she saw Nicholas. It has been a long time. He is now among the deceased. That is the official term. Unofficially he is dead as a doornail, done for, killed, cut open. He was not, officially, Joan's lover. You don't mean that. Get it right. He was her lover only in an official sense. That's more like it.

One could be out on the town. Picture it: the dance floor crowded with shimmyers and twisters, the mirrored globe spinning checkered light above their heads, the pop of champagne corks in the background, Joan with a glittering spray of confetti in her hair, dancing with strangers, because she can take it, she can take anything. There she is, dancing in sequined black, letting the old and the newest grief—you are not saying grief, that's not a word you want to look at—letting the music, then, energize her swayings and her spins. Or if that seems too much, too youthful, too hopeful, picture her in a quiet cushioned piano bar for the sophisticated late-night drinker, not huddled in this apartment, with its efficient geometries, drinking alone, facing the facts.

So face them: Nicholas has been murdered. He was a prostitute.

He believed in Puccini. He was not a doctor. Joan's father was a doctor who touched naked people with his hands, professionally, for money. The doctor believed in love at first sight and Shakespeare. He got hepatitis and died before Joan finished high school. He had a beautiful wife who attended charity balls and looked after the best interests of their only child. The doctor's wife believed in wishing upon a star and marrying for money. She died in a car crash when her daughter was twenty-two.

According to the newspaper, Nick's throat was cut by a jealous lover who mistook him for somebody else.

One is supposed to understand that Joan takes none of this personally, correct? That is correct. Consider the alternatives. Weeping, howling, for hours, for days, beating the breast, tearing the hair, these are things people do. And there is rending, there is laying waste. One could make mincemeat of the father's record collection, all that mystifying moonlight in Vermont. One could smash the porcelain dressing-table equipment, the mirror, the brush, the comb, the exquisite containers for cosmetics and jewelry, the adornments of womanhood all bestowed by the mother, all costly and fragile. Why not reduce to mournful rubble that vase, a gift from Nicholas, with its whooping crane arched and aflutter as it dances the mating dance? Because nothing would change, there would be no second chance, nothing that would make any difference, only debris everywhere and that unavoidable moment when one would reach for the broom and the dustpan, then vacuum the remains that refused to be swept. Imagine the hum of the vacuum as it finished them off, once and for all.

No, don't. Instead, tell yourself a little story: the one about the doctor and the doctor's wife, and how one night their daughter approached the closed French doors of their bedroom to tell them that she had been asked to dance at the cotillion, that the other girls had admired her dress, that the lights in the ballroom had made her giddy and desirable, that she had let one of the boys do it to her in his car. And in the story the daughter stands outside the bedroom doors and sees the doctor and the doctor's wife stretched out on their huge bed, reading novels under soft light, in their salmon-colored silk pajamas, in their enchanting room, enormous and golden. She is one of them now, she thinks. And when she finally catches her father's eye and mouths the words "may I come in," the two of them are instantly in cahoots—belle of the ball and dashing doctor exchange a look of playful defiance against the reading woman who wanted French doors for the bedroom, who wanted her daughter never to approach when the doors were shut, and who got whatever she wanted. So despite the cahoots, the dashing doctor waves away his grown-up child in her fairytale dress and she waves back, happy to comply, devoted to his devotion.

One could leave it at that, without compunction—it is perfectly understandable, the need to make things up, put words in people's mouths, reinvent the dead. Why not take one's cues from those bad books about a changeling or a cowboy rescued in the final episode by a rosy-cheeked family of ten or a whore with a heart of gold? No one else would have to know the real story.

But you know. And you must note the difference between one thing and another. The cotillion, for example, was real, as was the admired dress and the fucking in a car with somebody named Johnny or Bob who laughed the whole time. Standing outside the bedroom door, that was real. But the doctor who had once been dashing was not dashing then. He was yellow and he was dying and no one was saying that she loved him at first sight. And there were no French doors, no way to see inside, to see them together on the huge bed, beneath those lights, inside that room which was in fact enormous and golden, but was not in fact enchanting. It was not the room but the doctor's wife that was enchanting. That was true. And it was true that the father and the daughter would do whatever she wanted. They would do it for her creamy skin and her exotic eyes, for the way she looked in chiffons and furs, for the spells she cast with her apologies and atonements.

You remember the gawky little girl in too frilly a pinafore holding hands with her glamorous mother on a windy night. They were walking and it was dark and her mother was singing "S'Wonderful" as if it were a lullaby, holding her little girl's hand so meaningfully that nobody paid any attention to the crack of the first broken knuckle, nor the second, and it did not occur to Joan to say I think you're hurting me as her knuckles snapped and broke, one by one, the spell was so intimate and thick, her mother's gold bracelets so dazzling. *You can't blame me for feeling amorous.*

On the contrary, one could blame her, one ought to blame her, since that was only a dream, or mainly a dream. The lullaby was true, and the hand-holding, and the bracelets: they belong in the record. The rest didn't happen.

Other things happened. One could say without bending the truth that Joan cracked and broke when she was twenty-one and her mother said, "You live too much like a monk, my darling," and then, "Your womanhood will be a disaster if you're no good in bed." One might have held one's ground, argued that living like a monk had its advantages. Vaguely perceived dangers were being avoided. Keeping a grip on oneself was being accomplished. Somebody had to do it.

But somebody also let that "my darling" work its magic, let herself hear wonderment in her mother's word "womanhood," let herself hear valor, ritual self-control, a tale of trials cleverly withstood. Somebody gave in to the dazzling suggestion that an afternoon of professional instruction might change her life, might make her s'marvelous.

It did not occur to you to say, I think you're hurting me. You agreed without a peep to let your mother make the inquiries, set up the appointment. You wanted it. Not love. Womanhood. Afterwards you thanked her. That's all.

But that's not all. You didn't tell her that he held your face in his hands, pressed your cheek against his cheek, that he smiled into your smile like a prince of the desert who knows the wonder of water and knows where to find it.

You didn't tell her the things he said, didn't describe the worn tapestry textures of his old Florentine voice. He said, "In these rooms, we do not fuck." He said, "Without romance, we are nothing." He said, "Sometimes, with the ladies, they weep when I make love with them, and this is a sadness I do not wish to know."

But he did know. And he was not the right man, but they killed him, cut him open. He was not a young man, but they mistook him for one. Correction: there was no "they." According to the newspaper, there was one man and he was captured and he was reported to have said that even though he got the wrong man, he was satisfied.

That first time, when you met, you said to him that you were not a virgin, and he said to you that he did not think of himself as a whore.

And later, the last time you saw him, he said, "I have been waiting for you. I did not know that I was waiting. We think that we can outsmart it, but we are wrong." You said nothing instead of everything. And then he said, "I can wait." But Nick is at the morgue tonight, in a drawer, with a tag attached to one of his toes.

You have been there before, to the morgue. Descended the concrete steps to the basement, steady, resolute, you could take it. You didn't hesitate at the heavy door, you pushed it open, didn't wait for the coroner to play the gentleman, you pushed it open and went inside, imagining the smell of the prepared and pickled dead.

What else did you do? You looked at your beautiful mother and the driver of the car. Your mother was almost recognizable. Almost. So was her companion.

You had seen him once before, on the day she drove you to the Beverly Hills Hotel for your appointment with Nicholas. It was one o'clock in the afternoon and the fog had still not lifted. On the way to the hotel, at a stoplight, a young man in jeans and cowboy boots stuck a lurid beckoning tongue out at your beautiful mother. Tonguing the air as if he were tonguing her. Pinning her to the seat with his gesture that seemed to you not disrespectful but tender, and as full of promise as the blush that moved over the glorious skin on your mother's neck, spreading upward toward those eyes whose gaze was a dark quicksand.

One has made room, with the quicksand stuff, for some crude pun about the would-be sucker sucked in, drowned in the moist grit of those killer eyes.

Stick with the facts, Joan. As in: it was the same young man in the jeans and the cowboy boots who a few months later was driving the sports car that cracked up on the treacherous Pasadena freeway. It was on the local news, right after a story about Eddie Fisher and Elizabeth Taylor. The crash was newsworthy because it held up traffic for two hours, in the dark, in the rain. The newscaster described the stationary line of headlights as "spellbound." She would not have wanted it any other way—Joan's mother, that is.

At the morgue Joan was told that the driver of the car was carrying a union card that identified him as an actor. The coroner wanted to know if her mother was also in the business. "Oh yes," she had said. "We're a show business family." Well done, Joan. Why not make yourself another drink? Good idea.

Your father used to drink vodka gimlets. At his funeral your mother wanted you to speak, so you spoke. You said things that were made up. You don't remember what you said. You didn't want to tell about the time he had tried to reassure you by saying, in the voice of an amateur Shakespearean player, "Evidence to the contrary notwithstanding, your mother is quite taken with me. Quite." You didn't want to tell that he had been lost to the world for a long time, slain in the ancient way, magnificently, by Cupid's arrow. You kept him to yourself.

Kept the mother too, didn't you? but without the strain of a public appearance. You had her cremated, quick, didn't attend the service, let the assembled mourners say out loud that Joan was too stricken with grief—they would use that word—and let them say in private that Joan was too ashamed, too embarrassed, poor Joan. You told no one—that's not true, you told Nicholas, you told him everything—that, since no one else did, you claimed the young actor's body, had him buried in a prime spot in a Hollywood cemetery where the stars are buried. You arranged for a permanent display of American Beauties at the gravesite, and eventually dug your mother's ashes into that bed of roses.

And what did Nicholas say to you? He said, "We have a dignity. We are not animals. They can't take that away." And what did you say to him? "They can take anything they want."

Look at the photograph in the newspaper. He is lying face down, covered by a gaudy striped beach towel, in the parking lot of the hotel. Two policemen are standing beside the body, saying something to each other, smiling. Look at them. Do not get up from your chair, get your scissors, and cut their heads off. Those smiles belong in the record. You know that.

And you know that you ought to have thrown a party, decorated the bar with balloons and streamers, tossed out the newspaper, filled the mating crane vase with purple lilies. You ought to have seduced a jolly professor of economics, performed your womanhood with skill and grace, left the man weeping with uneasy pleasure, then returned to your guests, poured champagne, and proposed a toast to the deceased instructor.

With whom it was supposed to have been strictly business. But the daughter of the doctor and the doctor's wife found herself smiling into his smile, pressing her cheek against his cheek while their hands unbuckled and unbuttoned that first time and all the times thereafter, when it should have been strictly business, when he shouldn't have been telling her a love story, shouldn't have spoken of lips and eyes and honey, the sweetest dreams, whispering as if his body were inventing the words he whispered, as if the young woman he were making love to made such invention possible, as if the pasts they gradually revealed to each other intended them only and always for that present, for dancing in the dark, bare feet on the golden carpet, for that lagoon of a bed, the blue-green sheets, her fingertips along his spine, his thighs, the two of them swimming, gliding around and over and into each other as if they were born to the water, as if they believed in everything.

But you never forgot to slide a check under the dish of mints on the coffee table, on behalf of strictly business. And you did not forget to get a grip on yourself on the night, months later, when he finally displayed all the uncashed, undeposited checks—you held on tight as he ripped them up, turned them into snowflakes, confetti, stardust. On behalf of strictly business, you tried to look away when he smiled as if he knew you were at last a goner, as if a happy ending might come true, as if you were ready to press your palms onto his, mingling your fortunes.

No. You stood outside his door one last time, about to knock, about to enter and slip off your shoes, about to smile into his smile, and then you pushed away from it, made yourself decide that it will have been strictly business, that it will have been mission accomplished, that everything else belonged to a story that did not belong to Joan. And so you didn't knock, didn't enter, didn't respond to his calls, didn't go back.

But there is one more fact, isn't there? Say it.

The fact is, you might have, you wanted to, you could have, he was almost right, you were almost ready. Sooner or later you might have gone back, let yourself sink, magnificently, in the ancient way. This is true.

* * *

When Ernest returned to Los Angeles employed and relieved at twenty-nine—freed from the ordeal of living in the quaint claustrophobia of Cambridge, Mass., where it seemed that everything showed, all the small, stinging improprieties in his attire and his manners, his taste and his pocket-money—he rented rooms in a well-shaded two-story house in Santa Monica. The landlady, a spindly woman in her late sixties, never married, whose arrangement included breakfast and laundry, told him in no uncertain terms that she did not take boarders for the companionship but for the money.

There was space upstairs for two boarders, and so to ensure his privacy in the long run Ernest took both rooms, each laden with crocheted lap rugs whose odor of dried flowers, not unlike the odor of the landlady herself, was oddly, compellingly familiar, though there was no such thing as crocheted lap rugs and dried flowers in his background. The rooms were laden, too, with ceramic knickknacks. "I didn't buy a one of those," his landlady told him. "People think women want such things. And they'll expect to find them here when I die. So I keep them. What the hell." For the three years that he lived there, he was careful with all the things that belonged to her, as if they were his own.

She was the one who bailed him out of jail that time. He wasn't about to call his father, to confess within the cramped father-son arena to assault and battery, to the not just intense but unnamable pleasure he had taken in delivering a bone-breaking punch, a dead-on-target blood-spattering knuckle-bruising ferocious left to the asking-for-it jaw of the ex-marine, Korea vet, Boston-born, hoity-toity-talking sonofabitch who in a bar that night had called Ernest a queer.

If it hadn't been for the inescapable jail smells of piss and vomit and shit, for the drunken cellmates who crowded him, breathing nothing resembling breath into his face, he would have spent the night there, done his time proudly, and found a lawyer in the yellow pages in the morning. But he couldn't stomach it, the jailhouse camaraderie, and so he called his landlady.

On the way back to the house in her car, in which he took in that mysterious odor, a vanishing sweetness, he told her what had happened, and she told him how much money he owed her. Then she said, "Get one thing straight, kid. No use fighting city hall. Everybody's queer."

* * *

Love and Marriage

Joan and Ernest cut short their honeymoon trip to June Lake in order to attend his father's memorial service, which Ernest said was just as well—"He couldn't have timed it better"—since the fish weren't biting, not at his line, in any case, and having a wife who could catch two or three keepers without thinking it through would take some getting used to.

"These trout are like everybody else," he'd said to Joan. "They go for the blonds. All you have to do is sit there." He managed to say this so that it sounded more like flattery than resentment—after all, they were newlyweds.

In the car, as they headed back to Los Angeles, Ernest said, "Maybe my mother will show up. The last time I saw her, she was a blond."

This was rare—a reference of any sort to the mother-who-left, who hadn't laid eyes on her son for almost fifteen years—and Joan wasn't sure what to do with it. She wanted to say the right thing, to be a clever and understanding wife. But there was this, too: if she encouraged Ernest to talk, helped him to open that particular lid, would she, in turn, be expected to speak about matters long since locked away? Maybe. It wasn't worth the risk.

So Joan waited for a while, let a silence settle before she said, "Would your father want her to show up?"

"He'd want the last laugh."

"What about you?"

"Like father, like son." This was his father's line—and they both knew it. But Ernest delivered it as if it were his own, and he was grateful for the grin on Joan's face, for the private joke they were sharing, and for her not pointing out that the joke was on him.

Joan had met Ernest's father a few weeks after her first encounter with Ernest—which from the word go had an unspoken decidedness about it, as if they had no choice but to marry, and which led them to visit the one still living, still locatable, still more or less amenable relative they had between them and announce their engagement.

Ernest's father's roommate, Charles, took on the role of host for this event, served the highballs and the assortment of nuts mixed with cereal. He did his best—his best was very good—to disguise his amusement. Ernest's father, shrunken and wispy-haired but nevertheless boyishly ruddy, kissed Joan's hand, told her to call him Jerry, and proclaimed without ado that she was making "a ter-ri-ble mis-take."

"I ne-ver see him," Jerry went on, speaking through the device that stood in for the larynx he'd lost to cancer. "My son the ge-o-lo-gist. He lives un-der-ground. Where it is qui-et."

Ernest sat apart on a stiff modern chair—a work of art, according to Charles—eating the nuts and the cereal, one handful after another, watching his betrothed take pleasure in his father's remarks. "Mar-ry me in-stead," he heard his father say to Joan. "Or Char-lie. Char-lie has a trust fund. He will take good care of you."

After the second highball, Ernest mentioned that he and Joan had met in a restaurant in Hollywood, that the wind had followed her through the door and lifted her skirt. "It was classic," Ernest explained, his posture momentarily boastful. "Irresistible."

Jerry shook his head. "Don't kid your-self. It was not the legs. It was the hair. Like fa-ther, like son."

Ernest was the only one who found this comparison absurd, the only one who laughed out loud, so that his laughter was all too memorable. He looked to Charles—he knew better, he looked anyway—to come to the rescue. But nothing doing. Ernest was on his own. He shrugged.

His father shrugged back, then added, "Char-lie's hair was ne-ver blond. That should tell you some-thing." Jerry aimed this bit of clarification at his son, then bestowed a wink on the bride-to-be, who was looking from father to son, son to father, bewildered by the paucity of physical resemblance between them, charmed by the penchant for playful fisticuffs—it was playful, wasn't it?—that seemed to run in the Warner blood. She wanted to be in the ring with them, perfect an agile stance—it was this, after all, in some sense, that had drawn her to Ernest in the first place. Wasn't it?

"He puts his mind on holes," Jerry said to Joan. "He will be-tray you. Mark my words. Caves and holes and dirt."

Joan sat next to the old man on the couch, admiring the remnants of his handsome face as he struggled one syllable at a time to give shape to speech. She squeezed his hand. "And rocks," she told him, raising an eyebrow, feigning man-to-man intimacy. "Ernest thinks about the pure insides of rocks."

Jerry returned the squeeze. "You are no rock, my dear," he said. "And you were no mai-den, ei-ther, when you a-greed to be-come a wife." He took such feet-kicking delight in this piece of incisiveness that Joan giggled like a schoolgirl, and Ernest motioned to Charles that he would refill his own drink, thank you.

Ernest turned his back on the others, determined to ignore both the uncharacteristic giggle—that's not *my* Joan—and the entreaty of his father who was rubbing it in, patting the vacant cushion on the couch, saying, "Sit here, son. Sit next to me." As in: I dare you to sit beside the dying body of your father, to sniff, to touch, heh heh.

Ernest stood at the bar, fussing, trying not to listen, trying to turn no response into a dare of his own—albeit secondary and flaccid. He put a fistful of nuts into his mouth, buried that last unutterable but not unthinkable word. Nonchalance was clearly in order, giving up without giving in. He returned to his chair and said, "You won't seduce her, Dad. She looks like a featherweight, but she's not. She's too tough for you."

Joan wanted to confirm this assessment in some fashion. She wanted to show some muscle, though she had no interest in belittling her future father-in-law, taken as she was by his decrepit sparkle, by that mediated voice laboring itself into mischievousness. So she said, to her fiancé, "And too tough for you, too, mister"—a confirmation that apparently pleased both father and son, and that elicited from Charles his only contribution to the banter. "That's the spirit!" he said to Joan.

It was in just such a spirit that this foursome stood a few months later, on a rainy April afternoon, in the office of the retired judge who had been hired to tie the knot.

Charles, in an exuberant mood, played the best man, carried the rings, poured champagne, and stood so close to Ernest that their shoulders touched, despite the groom's repeated attempts to disengage. Jerry held Joan's hand and performed a version of the father-of-the-bride.

"It is a mo-ther he wants," Jerry said to the judge. "Not a wife."

The judge put on his spectacles and gave Joan the once-over. "You don't look to me, young lady, like a mother."

"I'm not." Joan wondered what the judge thought a mother ought to look like. Or a bride, for that matter—though she assumed that her mocha-colored silk chemise and the bouquet of Easter lilies supplied by the fond and fastidious best man were convincing. "I'm a fisherman," Joan explained.

Ernest didn't respond to this tweak. Instead, he looked at Jerry. "I'd settle for a father," he said, convivially, swallowing any suggestion of complaint. But not deep enough.

"Count your god-damned bless-ings, son."

"That won't take long." Ernest chuckled, as if he'd gained the upper hand.

The judge, on the basis of Charles's bulk and his tender proximity to the groom, asked, "Aren't you the young man's father?"

"I'm the mother," Charles told him. "Of the other one." He waved a thumb toward his roommate.

"Of all of us, actually," said Joan.

"Lucky me!" Charles, beaming, gave the groom a pinch on the cheek.

Joan and Jerry clinked their glasses and drank champagne.

Ernest said, "Let's get this show on the road."

Joan wondered if Ernest remembered that he had said the same thing after the two of them had visited his father that first time. She had invited him up to her apartment, where they sat sipping vodka, one on each of the two loveseats, pretending not to recall a previous occasion—same place, same drinks—when Joan had begun to unbutton Ernest's shirt and he had stopped her, saying something about her having to meet his father first, as if his father were an obstacle she would have to get over in order to test herself, her durability. Once the meeting with the father had been accomplished and they were again in her apartment, Joan did not say that she had passed the test, that she had escaped not only intact but enthused. Enthused enough, it turned out, for her to hear a charming come-on in Ernest's voice when he finally set down his drink, this time began the unbuttoning himself, and said, "Let's get this show on the road."

In the judge's office, on the day of the wedding, nobody heard any charm.

Charles said, with an embellished salute, "Spoken like a stud at the gate, my dear boy!"

Jerry said, "I want to make a cit-i-zen's ar-rest!"

"Has there been a crime?" asked the judge.

"A-gainst ro-mance!" Jerry stomped his foot for emphasis.

Joan tried to reassure her almost father-in-law. "We're a modern couple," she told him. "We get things over with. Keep things simple." Indeed from the very beginning she had been surprised by how easy it was with Ernest to be two rather than one, to go through the same motions with him that she had long gone through with herself, by herself. Careful not to let things matter too much, no rocking the boat, no going for broke—she and Ernest had this in common.

"No-thing is ev-er o-ver with," said Jerry.

Joan whispered, "I know."

Ernest said, "Do it, Judge."

"There should, at least, be a song," said Jerry. "Char-lie, sing "Love and Marriage."

Charles obliged this request with the line: "*You can't have one without the uuhh-ther.*"

Ernest looked at Joan—that is, gave her a look—and she said precisely what he needed her to say. "Do it, Judge."

"I am afraid we have lost her, Jerry," said Charles.

"A-las!"

The judge cleared his throat, as if this group might be called to order. "Ernest Warner, do you take—?"

"Yes."

"No chan-ces," said Jerry.

"Joan Stuart—?"

"I do."

"Well spoken!" Charles applauded. "Brilliantly bride-like!"

Joan curtsied a thank you.

"Exchange the rings and so forth," said the judge, apparently thinking it best to be quite modern, get this over with.

Jerry nudged the bride. "Holes and dirt. Think it o-ver."

"I'm not good at that," Joan told him.

"Get good at it."

Ernest loosened his tie and drank the champagne that Charles offered him.

"…power vested in me by the state, et cetera, I now pronounce you man and wife. You may kiss the bride."

Which is what Ernest's father did, immediately, and with a grand, old-fashioned flourish.

Joan learned at the memorial service that Ernest's father had known for some time the whereabouts of the mother-who-left: the wife who one day boarded a Greyhound bus and never returned, who wound up in Paris, who never divorced him, nor he her, and for whom funds had been set aside to assure her participation in the "festivities of grief," as Jerry put it in a note that crossed the Atlantic two weeks before he died.

Joan learned these things from the lady herself, the former Anne Warner, now Dominique Adams, artiste and part-owner of a small cafe on the Left Bank, who greeted her sullen son with a European kiss on both cheeks and a preemptive response to rumors. "Contrary to everything you may have heard—does she or doesn't she?—your mother is not a full-fledged lesbian."

"I've heard nothing," Ernest told his mother, whose seemingly unbruisable physique matched his own.

"And this exquisite thing must be the bride!" Dominique linked an arm through Joan's in the manner of an enthusiastic sorority sister.

"Yes," said Ernest. "The full-fledged bride." He wandered away from the two women as if there were something else he meant to do.

"The pause that refreshes," said his mother. "Very well then. He leaves us, poor thing, to introduce ourselves."

"I'm Joan."

"Of course you are. And I am Dominique, the wayward wife, the wanderer, the whatever else they may have told you about me. I confess to it all, and I absolve myself *tout suite*."

"They've told me almost nothing."

"Secretive as ever, are they? I'd hoped poor Ernest might have loosened up along the way."

"He didn't," said Joan. "Why do you call him 'poor' Ernest?"

By way of answering this inquiry Dominique swept her free hand through the air and directed Joan's gaze toward her husband, who in fact had nothing to do, who was standing by himself, in the shade. And no question about it, Ernest—whose colors were browns and blues, who never wore black, who rarely wore sunglasses—looked in the just-purchased suit and the sunglasses he'd borrowed from his wife like a third-rate actor who'd forgotten his lines. Yes, Joan had to agree, poor Ernest.

"The beard is a wonderful touch," said his mother. "Too bad he doesn't look a thing like his father."

"He does not want to be doing this," said Joan, checking herself, not saying "we," we don't want to be doing this, or worse, I don't want to be doing this. I want Jerry to be living. I don't want to be left to my own devices.

"See me, you mean, after all this time."

"I mean this occasion," said Joan.

"Ah, the burial of the beloved father!"

"Jerry was cremated."

"Literal-minded, are we? Not to worry. You'll get over it. Everything can be gotten over in time."

"I'll miss him," Joan said. "In any case."

"Between us"—Dominique managed an air of confidentiality without lowering her voice—"he would have lived longer if that roommate of his had been a genuine queer, *n'est-ce pas*? I know my husband. A romantic through and through. He needed a lover, of any stripe, not a nursemaid. Men can be so jejune, don't you think?"

"Charles loved him." Joan said this as if she were certain. She did not say that there was certainly nothing jejune about either Jerry or Charles. Ernest, perhaps, was another matter. And Joan herself, at the moment, felt exceedingly jejune.

She looked over at her husband, who seemed to be having a change of heart, who was making his way back to them. He stopped along the way to have his hand grabbed by a tall man wearing a black cape.

"You can't trust an ascetic," said Dominique. "It's unnatural."

"Charles isn't—"

Dominique gave her daughter-in-law's arm a pat to signal end-of-that-line-of-conversation. "The son returns!" She put her hands on Ernest's bearded cheeks. "I am merely a dabbler, *mon fils*."

Ernest removed her hands from his face. "I have no interest in your sex life. Whatsoever."

"You're a hard man, McGee."

"My mother," Ernest explained to Joan, "quotes the radio."

Joan had to admit that she was in over her head. "Why don't I help Charles greet the guests," she murmured, and left mother and son to do the renegotiating on their own.

It would not have surprised her, however, that Ernest was not in the least inclined to renegotiate, to re-anything. In fact, what he wanted was to give his mother an enduring dose of indifference. What he wanted was for her to depart, pronto. What he wanted was a drink. He did not like her abundance of bracelets, her thick blond curls that had begun to unravel from the modest widow's bun, or the sound of her voice—rusty with drawn-out conversations.

Dominique said, "People change. It is all truth or consequences. Life. Everything. You are old enough to know this."

"Yep," said Ernest. He wished he were wearing that black cape.

"Thirty, yes?"
"Thirty-two."
"There, you see? A grown man."
"Yep."
"Your father and I, we were young. Inexperienced. Neither of us had even been to a movie when we met. We knew nothing."
"Nope."
"You are aware, I presume, that we remained married all this time."
"Yep."
"We've kept, of course infrequently, in touch. Remained, in a few of the particulars, birds of a feather."
"Crows."
"Ooo la la! And what does that make our dear son?"
"Beats me."
"You have in mind something grand? An eagle perhaps?"
"Nope."
"What are you then? Say it."
"What difference does it make?"
"None," said Dominique. "I am not afraid to make myself clear. Your mother is known among her many friends and acquaintances for her relentless honesty."
"He didn't trust you. Dad didn't." Ernest almost winced at his clumsy—he hadn't whined, had he?—change of subject. But he held it in, didn't let her see anything but self-composure.
"There is nothing simple about marriage," Dominique replied. "You will know soon enough. Do you trust your bride?"
Ernest looked at Joan, who was standing next to the elegant Charles. The two of them were shaking hands with Jerry's drinking buddies, miscellaneous friends-of-friends, the old co-workers from Paramount.
Not known among his friends and acquaintances for his relentless honesty, Ernest said, "Yep. I trust her."
He waved then at his bride, gave her the a-okay sign, beckoned her to rejoin them, and produced a smile as she approached that was supposed to say that he hadn't let his mother get the better of him.
Joan thought he looked ill. She held his hand.
"My mother has become sophisticated," said Ernest.
"And have you, too, my son, become sophisticated?"
"Not a bit." Ernest laughed.

Dominique didn't laugh. She turned the question on Joan. "Has he?"

"Not a bit," said Joan.

Ernest opted to take this as a show of loyalty, as Joan's participation in his joke.

Dominique saw it otherwise. "You have chosen well," she said to Ernest. "This Joan of yours will sharpen your edges."

Ernest said out loud what Joan was thinking. "It's the other way around. I'll sharpen hers."

"Bravo then! A man of blunt instruments you turned out to be! I want to know all about it. Shall we go inside?"

"Inside" meant a banquet room at the Ambassador Hotel. Charles's idea: what one does when there is no funeral; when there are important guests from out of town (the important Dominique had brought with her one aging chanteuse and an adorable blond pixie of a waitress); when the deceased specifically requested a prayerless, wreathless, all-out bash; when he had stipulated platters piled high with ham sandwiches and peeled shrimp, fresh strawberries and oranges, a guest list that included total strangers, hundreds of yards of crepe paper, individually-wrapped party favors (sampler bottles of Chanel No. 5 and an array of hit singles, like Bobby Darin's "Mack the Knife" and Connie Francis's "Who's Sorry Now?"), and an enormous rum-laden punch into which his ashes might be surreptitiously sifted and stirred—and were.

Charles told Joan about it. "A brilliant bequest, don't you think?"

Joan raised her glass of punch and drank. "Will you tell the others?"

Ernest and his mother were seated at one of the linen-covered tables that framed the dance floor, making something like conversation, and drinking the punch, glass after glass.

"I think we ought to," Charles said.

"Jerry would want them to know."

"Precisely!"

"But not too soon."

"They must drink deep!" Charles took two more glasses of punch from the tray proffered by one of the tuxedoed waiters. "May I have the privilege of telling the mother?"

"She's all yours," said Joan.

"And you will inform the son?"

"When the time comes. I think I'll save it up. For a special occasion." For fisticuffs, Joan was thinking. Playful fisticuffs.

"He would do the same for you, my dear."

"I know," said Joan. "Ours is a marriage of true minds."

Charles laughed. "Jerry was right about you," he said. "You'll last."

Joan wasn't at all sure about that, but she was prepared to give it her best shot. She raised her glass and proposed a toast to lasting, and then to Jerry, and then to poor, dear Ernest.

Afterwards, when it was just the two of them, in what used to be Joan's apartment, the newlyweds sat apart on the loveseats. Joan was still wearing her black and white cocktail dress. Ernest had changed into comfortable khakis and a workshirt. There was a plate of food between them on the coffee table, leftovers from the memorial service, which was still going strong when Ernest decided that it was time for them to leave.

"She goes back tomorrow. To gay Parie." Ernest took a bite out of one of the ham sandwiches. "Forever," he added with his mouth full.

"The little waitress, Belinda, will be disappointed," said Joan.

"Her name is Bettina," Ernest said. "And she's staying."

"Oh." This did not seem to Joan a good time to echo Ernest's father, to mention caves and holes and dirt. Betrayal. There would never be a good time for that.

"Bettina wants to see the homes of the stars, Disneyland. I said I'd help her get a job, find a place to live."

"Does she fish?"

"She doesn't go near the water." Ernest finished his sandwich. "Can't swim."

"That's nice."

"Yes it is."

On the other hand, this *did* seem to Joan a good time, a special occasion, in honor of Bettina's decision to stay in Los Angeles, for revelations. "I want to tell you something," she said. "About the punch."

"I already know," said Ernest.

"You know?"

"Of course."

"Who told you?"

"Nobody."

"Charles wouldn't have told you. Did your mother?"

"Nobody told me." Ernest picked up another sandwich and took a big bite. "I could taste him," he said, chewing.

"You what?"

Ernest laughed. The defeated look on Joan's face made up for a lot of things—like those trout that she caught and he didn't, like his so-called mother's dabblings, like his father's guessing and saying out loud in public that the bride-to-be was no maiden, as if people had to know these things, as if it mattered one way or the other.

"I could taste him," Ernest said again, hefting the sandwich, delighted to repeat such a statement to such a woman, his very own blond, his bride, a keeper, heh heh.

* * *

After graduating from the business school at USC, Joan went to work for Bullock's, then for Magnin's, where she confounded them by refusing the offer of the chi-chi spot as buyer in the better dress department. Sportswear would keep her closer to home, she didn't like to travel, she wanted sportswear. They moved people around and gave her sportswear, with the understanding that they were the ones who wore the pants in the company family. But they suspected from the start—from the "first salvo," as it became known—that they were dealing with a world-class bitch.

They said so openly—the cuff-linked, class-ringed managers—told her about their suspicion in that "just kidding," cocky way of theirs. At the end of her first season, for the office party, they made a show of giving themselves kid gloves in order to drive home the hilarious point of her special treatment. Nobody laughed but them.

So they set out to get her goat, one-up her, make her demonstrate some fundamental female pettiness by taking all the credit for her successes. The thing is, she let them take all the credit, as if it didn't matter, as if she owned the place. Only it was worse because she didn't snub anybody, didn't look down her almost perfect nose, gave nobody a good reason to say behind closed doors that she ought to take her menstrual cycle elsewhere. They were at a loss.

"She has all the right instincts," said Manny.

"She has savvy that verges on acumen," said Jules.

"She's what'd'ya-call-it, nice," said David. Not friendly. They agreed that there was none of the usual friendliness. But they had to concede to "nice."

They tried to flush out the hidden weaknesses. David flirted, Jules fawned, Manny offered raises. Nothing worked. Joan went about her business like a team player who can't be bought. A regular Sandy Koufax, they told her. And she said something about his having just won his second Cy Young. Not even "award." Just "Cy Young." Jules told her he was "strictly-speaking awe-inspired." David started using peroxide, hoping to imitate her California look. Manny called a meeting that didn't include her.

At the meeting he began by telling the others what they already knew: that she was good, she almost never missed, she knew what sold and when and why and where. She was strictly business. Not only that, she seemed to know things they didn't know. It was uncanny. But he had a feeling—"And this does not go outta this room," he said. He had a feeling that underneath it all she was delicate, that she needed them to look out for her, that when they said among themselves "she has some kinda balls," they should never forget that they were speaking "you know, metaphorical."

*　　*　　*

Me and My Gal

Ernest learns from his wife that he's an exemplary pack rat. He doesn't say "that's news to me" because that's how Joan presents it, as news to him. What he does say is that he is not only exemplary, he's the best. Ernest has missed the point.

Joan says that it would *behoove* him to spend the afternoon sorting through whatever he keeps in his old trunk and those cardboard boxes he's been carting around for years.

Behoove my ass. Ernest grins at her attempt to lord it over him, embarrass him into disencumbering action. He appreciates the care with which she goes on to suggest that his hanging-on and hoarding is not manly. But he doesn't buy it. He assumes that his wife must be envious of his load.

So he is not displeased that the subject has finally come up. He's been wanting to show her his stuff, but didn't want to push it on her, took her silence about the boxes to mean disinterest. Envy was another matter. Envy he could handle. This is going to be fun. He'll save the contents of the trunk for last.

Ernest pours a couple of beers into the mugs he stores in the freezer and hands one to his wife. He's never seen her wear those dainty white gloves that women wear, but he likes the idea, wishes she had a pair for this occasion. Joan handling his stuff with those gloves on. Lace around the cuffs, pearl buttons. Later, she'd wear them to bed.

Ernest is smiling as he pulls the trunk from the hall closet and arranges the boxes in a semi-circle in front of the couch. He feels large, sexy. He feels like grabbing his crotch, giving his meat a friendly salute. But he doesn't do it. Not in front of Joan.

She might take it the wrong way. You never know with her. Most of the time he can live with that, sure. At the moment, he doesn't want to take any chances. As far as sex goes, he hasn't figured out if Joan is skittish or a know-it-all, and he doesn't want to. It's okay with him that they don't do it often. He likes the build-up, the sense of adventure. He likes thinking of himself as a jack-in-the-box. Pop goes the weasel!

Ernest can imagine giving his crotch a hearty handshake in front of some other woman. He can imagine doing a lot of things. But there is no one in front of whom he would rather display his accumulations. One item at a time. Piling up the stuff. A kind of reverse strip tease. Three decades' worth of treasures. Joan wouldn't be an easy audience. But that's the point.

What the hell. He gives the old equipment a contented jostle. But Joan doesn't seem to notice. She gets up and brings a garbage pail into the living room.

Ernest sees her doing this all her life. Even as a little girl, with maybe her little sleeves rolled up, she'd be big on spring cleaning, starting from scratch. No memorabilia, no clutter. Her room a virtual hermitage. Oiled woodwork, a smooth white bedspread, a small lamp, a lovely goldfish in a crystal bowl on the dressing table. It occurs to him that he might have liked it there, in such a room.

As far as he knows, Joan has no keepsakes. Just the one photograph of her parents, framed in sterling, there on the mantle. Movie star types—too good-looking, too wealthy. As luck would have it, they were both dead by the time he met their daughter. The sizing-up would have gone badly, no question. Not that his folks, while they were still more or less in the picture, were any joy ride. But Joan can handle herself. She makes a good impression. Sometimes too good. It's better this way—nobody in the picture but the two of them. Me and my gal. A couple of tough hombres.

What got to him the first time he laid eyes on her—that would be about four years ago, when she walked into that restaurant wrapped in a hot gust of wind—was the raw look on her face that seemed to be saying she wanted to crawl inside him and hide out until the whole thing died down. She gave him only a few seconds' worth of that look before she got hold of herself. But it was enough for him to see himself as some kind of he-man, a hero who could defeat the wind, the heat, the fear, you name it. Which of course he wasn't. And which of course she wasn't going to admit she needed, ever. So they were bound to hit it off.

Ernest sits next to Joan on the floor, between the couch and the boxes, and proposes a toast to ball-busters. Joan doesn't drink to that. She starts to open a box that is clearly marked **1950s**. It figures. Joan is tidy, but she's not systematic. Chronology? Forget it.

Ernest knows enough to know that chronological order has the same appeal to his wife as maps, rulers, recipes, scales—which is to say, no appeal. He finds it curious that she doesn't get lost, draws straight lines, makes a perfect soufflé, knows just about how much things weigh from the look of them. But he likes this about her. He enjoys finding her curious. He tells her now and then that she belongs in a ye olde curiosity shoppe. This is an endearment. Better hush than mush, that's his motto. When he suggests that they begin at the beginning, with the **1930s** box, Joan gives him a whatever-you-say-dear shrug. Ernest continues to smile, happy about the way this is going to go—which is to say, his way.

He pretends that he has forgotten what is contained in the first box. He is amazed, he says. He is flabbergasted. What is *this*? Can it be? Has he in fact hung on all these years to the grade school essays for which his penmanship was praised? I'll be damned.

It goes without saying that the essays are not garbage, so Ernest doesn't say it. And he doesn't tell his wife that he remembers wanting to be better than the other boys at something, anything, even hand-writing. And he was—better even, to everyone's surprise, than most of the girls. He shows the teachers' comments to Joan—who mimics, perfectly, his I'll be damned—and then places the essays on the couch, out of range.

Ernest is no fool. He lets his wife throw out an assortment of broken crayons, pencil stubs, and half-used unopenable bottles of glue. The two dozen tubes of craftsman's paint, all the colors, nearly new—that's another matter. Good stuff to have on hand, he says. Joan might want to make a sign, for instance. Or decorate eggs. Or teacups. Lined up side-by-side in the desk drawer, all these tubes, they'd be an inspiration. Joan knows what he's getting at, right? She shakes her head. Teacups? she asks. Ernest wants to be optimistic. Anything's possible, he tells his wife.

Joan lets him get away with this. He wouldn't have blamed her for laughing out loud, calling his bluff. But she's a good sport, most of the time. Ernest watches her reach into the box and gather up his old boy scout uniform. She shakes it out, volunteers to run it through the wash, and suggests that they give it to the Salvation Army.

He pictures her standing at the kitchen sink, a white apron tied around her waist, washing his old uniform, by hand. Ironing the yellow scarf until it is crisp and attentive. He has never actually seen Joan wash anything by hand. She rarely irons. He wants to tell her that she would look good doing these things. Restful and content. Almost cute. Instead, he tells her that he wants to make the uniform a personal gift, find some young boy to pass it on to, personally. He says that he'll keep an eye out for the right size boy.

As Joan sets the uniform aside, Ernest hands her a stack of comic books. Look, he says. This is what is meant by mint condition. Joan asks if in fact he read them. She says that they do not appear to have been touched. Ernest loves his wife for asking this question. *Every single one*, he gets to say. I read every one of them, *carefully*. This is how you acquire a collector's item. With *care*.

Joan says uh huh. She keeps digging. She comes up with a cigar box half-filled with old keys. A collector's item this is definitely not. But before she can recommend its disposal, Ernest tells her that you hang on to old keys because at one time or another they did something for you—got you in or out, got you on the road by car or skate, kept something safe for a little while. You don't throw such a thing away. Ernest is surprised that he repeats verbatim the explanation his father had used.

He was five or six when his father came into his room and presented him with the cigar box, decorated on its snug lid with a portrait of cigar-smoking men who appeared to be wearing women's clothing. And it was a genuine presentation—complete with whispered voices and ceremonial bows. You are the keeper of the keys now, his father had said. They're not good for anything but remembering, and that's everything. Ernest himself didn't have any keys at the time, useless or otherwise. But he felt the weight of what he'd been given—the promise the keys lived up to, or didn't, and the sadness in his father that he didn't want to have anything to do with but did anyway through no fault of his own.

Not long after the presentation of the keys young Ernest had heard his father talking to himself in the bathroom, apparently addressing the reflection in the mirror. You're lousy company, he was saying. Look at you. Go find yourself somebody to talk to. Ernest hid, expecting the bathroom door to swing wide open, expecting the search to begin right away, as though there weren't a moment to lose. But it wasn't like that. The door didn't swing open. His father kept talking. This is no good, young Ernest heard him say. Be a man. Get a grip on yourself.

Ernest thinks he might pass the keys on to the same boy, the potential boy scout, depending. The kid would have to show some gratitude—a lot of it. He asks his wife to bring them a couple more beers. He watches her leave the room, her wiry body that looks so good in pants. He wants a shot of whiskey with his beer, but he'll let it wait. For now, he puts the childhood essays, the boy scout uniform, the comic books, and the keys back into the **1930s** box and closes the lid.

Joan returns with the beers and two shots of whiskey. She has read Ernest's mind. What a wife. This is exactly how it's supposed to be. This is *excellent*. In her honor, Ernest decides to forego the chronological progression. He opens the remaining boxes, displays the goods. The rocks and the arrowheads, the marbles and report cards, the junior high and high school yearbooks—year after year the same moody eyes avoiding a direct look at the camera. Ernest regards this as a triumph over the system. He says he'd like to have seen Joan's school pictures, seen how she managed the ritual exposure. Same as you, she tells him. Sideways. Not, she adds, like this. She holds up a snapshot of Ernest's father standing in front of the movie studio where he worked as a go-fer all those years, smiling at the camera as if he had invented the California sunshine. Ernest tucks the snapshot back into one of the yearbooks. We, on the other hand, he tells his wife, live in the real world.

They turn to the collection of minerals and compasses and magnets—early tools of the trade. Joan is vaguely interested, with the emphasis on vaguely. This comes as no surprise. She has never been inquisitive about Ernest's profession, what got him started, what he does when he does a geological survey, what the difference is, say, between fluvial processes and continental drift.

No problem. This way, Ernest gets to keep something to himself. It helps him think of his work as a kind of magic, an art that can't be casually revealed in chit-chat at the end of the day over cocktails. Joan's pursuits are another matter. The retail business—culottes and v-necks, next year's swimsuit line, purchase orders and invoices, blah blah blah. When she talks about it over cocktails, he listens, and he imagines himself some twenty years hence, a graying wizard, whisking off his superbly-dressed wife in a chartered plane that carries them to Glacier Lake, where they stand hand-in-hand at the edge, she visibly moved and amazed, he all-knowing and benevolent.

Joan is looking through a stack of cheesecake and pin-up calendars from the forties and fifties—hips and breasts and polka dots, cheerleader smiles, the good old days. Ernest feels magnanimous. He says that she can throw them all out if she wants to, send them to the dump. But she doesn't want to. Research, she tells him. She'll take them to her office. Ernest suggests that it might not *behoove* her to keep them.

She ignores this remark and turns to the next item, the newspaper clippings: headlines and editorials, reports and recountings all carefully pasted onto thin sheets of blue construction paper that had been stapled into two thick batches, one marked WAR, the other SCIENCE. Joan wonders out loud what teenage Ernest did for fun. It's staring her right in the face, but she asks anyway. As if there had to be more to it. As if there had to be hamburger joints and girl-chasing and driving around. As if there had to be chaos. Ernest reminds his wife that her husband is an unusual kind of guy. She knows this, of course, and has sometimes commented upon it, sometimes admiringly. So what difference does it make that at the moment she thumbs through the clippings and says nothing?

As a rule, Ernest doesn't think about what sorts of admiring things Joan might have said to the man she has acknowledged as a "prior experience" but has never discussed. Oh baby oh baby oh don't stop. She wouldn't have. Not Joan. Granted, Ernest doesn't know what the guy had to show for himself. Besides the obvious. And he wouldn't mind hearing some of the details if the gist of the story were that the guy turned out to be a dud, a pansy, a dirty rat. The good thing is, Joan acts as if whatever it was never happened. Ernest is the same way about the women he slept with before he met his wife: like the bombshell graduate student secretary who kept a list of all of her conquests; or the top-heavy resident over at Cedar Sinai he'd made it with on a regular basis until she tried to get him into the sack with herself and another man. The point is, who cares? Ernest doesn't, you can bet on it.

He hands his wife some of his old books: Crane and London, Norris and Farrell. Joan asks if she can read them, says she'll be very very careful. She calls them his boys' books. Ernest laughs and pictures her in bed, reading *Call of the Wild*, wearing flannel pajamas decorated with choo-choo trains and cowboys, forgetting to finish the glass of milk and the peanut butter cookie because she has lost herself in a struggle for survival against an arctic blizzard, she and man's best friend.

Joan holds the books in her lap. She isn't kidding. She intends to read them. Ernest is beaming. It's time to get to the trunk. He pushes some of his things out of the way, downs his shot of whiskey, pulls the trunk into position, and then unfastens the clasps. The trunk is bursting with protective wads of newspaper. He tosses a wad at his wife. She nabs it, one-handed.

Ernest finds the book close to the top, just where it's supposed to be. He removes the rubber bands and the expertly-folded butcher's paper. It's a worn, fragile, illustrated book of Roman myths. A bookmark still indicates the page that matters: the fabulous depiction of Vulcan, fatherless and fiery metalworker tossed out of Heaven by the fickle queen mother who bore him, some say, to prove a point (I, too, can conceive a child without a partner). Joan appears to be impressed. And rightly so.

As he sets aside the remaining wads of newspaper, Ernest explains that Vulcan is the guardian of his models, the impetus when he was seventeen for a summer spent making miniatures of Fuji and Vesuvius and Kilauea. He lifts the plastic covering from the models. There has been no damage, no dust. They look the way they looked when he first made them, ominous and beautiful. Steep-coned, snowcapped, priestly Fuji—elegant and restful. Kilauea at war with itself, bleeding ribbons of molten lava over a landscape already killed and blackened. And Vesuvius, all shoulders and muscle, flexed above the Bay of Naples, still digesting the feast that was Pompeii. Ernest holds up each model, then places them one by one atop the cardboard boxes that surround his wife. He tells Joan that Vulcan led him to volcanoes and volcanoes led him to her. She smiles, at last.

There is one more thing in the trunk. A jar filled with chunks of rock-like mud. The jar is labeled with a wide strip of adhesive tape, in Ernest's praiseworthy nine-year-old script, **Death Valley**. Joan picks it up and says, this is just what we need. A jar of dirt.

Ernest leans back against the couch. His wife is too good to be true. He has heard no mockery in her voice. He sees no telltale signs of it lingering in her eyes or around her mouth. She apparently means it: this is just what we need. Ernest has never mentioned Derek, but she says it as if Derek were in her bones.

Derek: who hated the term babysitter as much as young Ernest did. Who called himself, not the babysitter, but The Sandman. It was Ernest's father who had arranged for Derek. It was Derek who showed Ernest the ropes, took him places—the tar pits, the racetrack, the observatory, the shipyards. No sissy stuff. They went to places meant for men. They went to Death Valley. Derek was a sophomore then at Occidental, driving out to the desert at top speed during Christmas break. He was fed up, he'd said, with all the seasonal decor. What the two of them needed was some *desiccation*.

Ernest didn't know what desiccation was exactly, but he was old enough to know what it felt like to be fed up. He couldn't have put it into words, the way Derek could. But that didn't matter. Derek wasn't interested in conversation. Conversation was for teenage girls and mothers. Derek just said things. The kinds of things Ernest figured he'd say someday, if he felt like saying anything at all. Derek said what they needed was some *nothingness*. As they came through the teeth of the Panamint mountain range and took in the miles and miles of cracked and overcooked desert, Derek said *shazam*. He said now *this* is what I call *Christmas*.

They found an oversize jar in the trunk, along with some rags they tied around their brows, like pirates. Ernest carried the jar and a crowbar, Derek a canteen and a compass, and they walked a blistered stretch of the valley as if it belonged to them, their shoulders back and their strides wide. Ernest didn't want it to end, ever. They searched for bones and snakeskins, but found none worth keeping, none that measured up to the aura. Before they left, Ernest used the crowbar to dig up a jagged patty of burnt mud, then he knocked it into pieces that would fit in the jar. Derek said that is just what you need. A *memento mori*. Something a man keeps on his desk. A *reminder*.

On the way back to Los Angeles in the late afternoon they kept all the windows rolled down, let the chilly air try, just try to make them shiver. Not a chance. They'd gone to hell and come back out again. Derek said that, as soon as he graduated, he was going to join the navy. Get acquainted with *rigor*. Get a tattoo. Ernest tried not to think about life without Derek.

At home, he showed the jar to his mother and said I'm keeping this. You're not throwing it away. He positioned it in the center of the table that served as a desk in his room. Kept it there until he went off to college, to Occidental. Even after Derek was killed in the war, the *memento mori* didn't do what it was supposed to do. Instead, it reminded Ernest of *shazam*.

The best part is that there's no need to tell any of this to Joan, who is surrounded by his things, who with one hand is touching his beautiful Fuji. Like Derek, Joan knows just what we need, and she isn't afraid to come right out and say so. There she is, cradling his boys' books in her lap, turning his stuff into her stuff. Oh baby oh baby oh don't stop.

* * *

 Ernest bought a gun in Chinatown, a week before he and his wife moved to Palm Springs. A heavy old Colt-45. For snakes. There were of course plenty of snakes in the Los Angeles hills. But there would be more of them in the desert.
 When he got home, his wife told him that she heard on the news about a man named Norman who took his little girl—she couldn't have been more than two—this man named Norman carried his daughter to the steps of the Pentagon, where he doused himself with gasoline, holding the little girl with one hand and dousing himself with the other, recklessly, so that she too got soaked, and people started yelling at him, "Drop the child!" But nobody went near him, they just stood back and kept on yelling "Drop the child!" and it was making Norman mad because they weren't listening to his statement of protest against the war in Vietnam. They kept yelling at him, "Drop the child!" Nobody was listening, so he finally dropped the child, let her fall there onto the steps, and somebody ran and picked her up, got her out of there. But nobody got Norman out of there, nobody—he made his speech, he was a Quaker, he lit the match.
 His wife didn't talk much about what she was afraid of, but she seemed to be terrified of this Norman, as if he posed some personal threat. Go figure, he said to himself. To his wife he said, "What's for dinner?"
 Fear of snakes was another matter entirely. At least his wife had enough sense to be as afraid of them as he was. The way they show up, always all-of-a-sudden there, too close, close enough to flick their tongues at the tender skin of your ankles. Out of nowhere. Like certain nightmares he had long since banished. Or worse: like memories of things that had never actually happened but might have, that he had to keep from happening, that seemed to be lurking around, wanting all of a sudden to happen.

Sometimes he wished that his wife were not afraid of snakes. That she would pick one up—maybe one of those colorful, harmless king snakes—and bring it to him, cooing and relaxed, as if it were no more than a kitten. And she would help him to touch it, to live through that. But that wasn't going to happen. So he was looking forward to shooting a few.

* * *

Someone to Watch over Me

This is how Joan remembers it.

She was alone in the Santa Ana wind. Listening to the tap of her heels on the sidewalk. Counting her steps. Thinking, do not give in.

Trash rolled down the street. Westwood was covered with dust. She heard the shop windows rattle. Her mouth tasted like the desert.

She knew the local weathermen were happy. On television they would show hair-raising photos of trees toppled onto cars and houses. They would make clever remarks about things gone with the wind. They would estimate the damages. Predict a sudden increase in suicide and domestic violence.

The wind followed her into the restaurant. She watched it blow against the hostess and against the man who'd been about to settle his bill. She saw the man's crisp dollars swept up by the hot gust. She saw the wind pushing at his sand-colored sports-coat. He was thick and bearded. He looked as if he intended to outlast everything.

She remembers some of the things that were said.
The hostess said, "Isn't somebody going to shut the goddamned door?"
The man didn't move, so Joan didn't either.
He looked at her and paid no attention to the wind.
They looked at each other as a waiter finally shut the goddamned door.
Joan's white skirt stopped billowing.
Someone else might embellish this recollection, linger on the fluttering white pleats, the unintended and suggestive exposure. But not Joan.
She remembers that she smoothed back the hair that had flattened against her damp face.
"The wind," she said, "is bad."
He said, "Of course, everything's bad."

His face was handsome. His grin was scary. She grinned too, watching herself follow his cues.

"You'd better buy me a drink," he told her.

They were standing side-by-side, waiting to be seated. He asked for a table near a window. She erased the image of herself hidden inside his soft jacket.

She remembers erasing this image, but not the image itself, which from the start was hazy, odorless. She remembers standing side-by-side and thinking of the steady click of her heels on the sidewalk. Saying to herself, do not let go. Count your steps. Control the deck.

He said Ernest.
She said Joan.
He said geology.
She said fashion industry.
He said it shows.
She said so does your geology.
He said I fold.
She said your deal.
He said I don't usually ask women to buy me a drink.
She said neither do I.
He said I was here for a meeting.
She said I used to come here with my father.

She remembers being pleased with the precision of her tone, given the imprecision of this last remark. The story it implied of a ritual intimacy, a colorful relationship, a tradition of Shirley-Temples-for-the-young-lady-and-we'll-both-have-the-clams. When in fact there had been only the one time. And by that time she was seventeen. Old enough to eat the clams and drink the Shirley Temple and mimic her father's brittle grace when he told her that he would soon die from something he caught from one of his patients.

Joan remembers the facts. October 1961. That would be 7 years ago. She was 25. She would finish her MBA in 6 months. She had lived in the same apartment for 4 years. There was no view there. She carried a $200 briefcase. Outside the restaurant it was 95 degrees. The wind was steady at 25 to 30 miles per hour, with gusts up to 50. There was 1 thing that she was sure of: she would not let herself hear the wail of her ghosts in the wind. It was 5:30 in the afternoon. It would be dark soon.

A paper umbrella came with her gin and tonic. She remembers opening and closing the umbrella.

The paper umbrellas are always the same. She does not need to remember what it looked like. She does not need to remember that Ernest's eyes made her think of a cliff, but she does anyway.

"You said everything is bad."

"The food here, for example," he explained.

"You said everything."

"Don't order the clams."

"You said of course."

"Because it's true."

"I know."

"I know you know. I saw you come in."

"You saw *everything's bad*?"

"I saw you."

She remembers overhearing part of an interview. A reporter asked a director if the shoot would take place on location. The director said, "I'm after a sense of conflagration. So I put my mind to it. I come up with fire. I come up with a villain who lets matches burn until they scorch his fingertips. I come up with a setting. I come up with it here, in these hills. This is where I locate the shoot. Make sure you quote me on that. Conflagration."

She heard this but did not turn to the reporter and set the record straight. Did not turn away from Ernest's stare and point out that the director did not invent California's crackling landscape. That he did not need to "come up with" fire. That fire, in fact, belonged to these hills. To the chaparral. To the sagebrush and bristlecone pine. To the needlegrass, the joshua trees, and the sharp-coned juniper that have to burn in order to flourish, and so welcome the lightning bolt and the arsonist.

She remembers that Ernest was watching her and that she was sweating.

He said, "I don't go to the movies."

"Me either."

"We have a lot in common."

"All I said was that I don't go either."

"You don't go because of the fakery. The flim-flam."

"The happy endings."

There was a pause. They drank their drinks.

"People in general are false," he said.
"Do you believe that?"
"I believe we've had this date with each other from the beginning."
"That sounds like a line from a movie."
"It is."

It was dark. The wind was pressing against the window. She heard no overhead music. No faint female voice singing *won't you tell him, please, to put on some speed, follow my lead*. None of that. But she felt a heaviness move in on her. Heavy enough to do damage. She was afraid because she didn't want to stop it. She told herself there was nothing complicated about this feeling. It was natural. And that is how she remembers it. As natural. And heavy enough to do damage.

Ernest said, "What are you afraid of?"
"The wind."
"What else?"
"I don't know."
"That sounds, to me, like everything."
"The wind dies down."
"So does everything." He seemed to be pleased with himself.
She remembers ignoring his smile. "The other thing I'm afraid of is memory."
"Forget it."
"Are you making a joke?"
"It's not what it's cracked up to be. It's fiction. It's not important."
"You can't forget memory."
"It pretends to be true, but it's not."
"You can try to control it."
"It's a cock-teaser. We want it to make us feel good, but it doesn't."
"You can try to keep it honest."
"And you fail."
"Not often," she told him.
"But you're afraid of failing."
"Aren't you?"
"To hell with it. And to hell with the wind."
"You can say to hell with it. And you can throw around words like of course. But that doesn't change the facts."
He said, "There aren't any. I was born here. I know."

At the time, she did not say I was born here too. And she did not mention the earliest scene she could remember. The one that took place in the enormous bedroom with a view of Griffith Park. Her mother was stretched out on the turquoise divan, wearing a golden silk peignoir. Telling her little girl about the dust storms that ruined the Midwest during the year of Joan's birth. Offering statistics and damage estimates. Showing illustrations from an old copy of *Fortune* magazine. Turning facts into omens.

Nor did she mention to Ernest another scene. The one she was imagining in which she was cooling her face against the hard fact of his abdomen.

She said, "Tell me something about rocks."
"Most of them are hard."
"Are you?"
"Sometimes. Now."
"I meant hard as in difficult."
"I know."
"Is this how people talk when they meet?"
"I have no idea."
"Me either."
"We think alike."
"Except you seem to be fearless."
"I'm not," he said. "I'm afraid of you."
"Good."
"So tell me something I should know."
"I was born during the year of the dust storms."
"That makes sense."
"It's meaningless."
"On the contrary," he told her. "The earth moved, of course, during those storms."

She remembers wanting to stand with that man at the edge of a cliff. They would ignore the pushing of the wind and the smell of smoke. They would be impervious and silent. She has no recollection of the look on her face when he said "the earth moved." But she knows that she did not laugh. He did.

He said, "Nineteen-thirty-six. When you were born, I was listening to The Shadow on the radio. *Who knows what evil lurks in the hearts of men? The Shadow knows.*"

"Did he?"
"Of course not."
"Did you know that then?"
"Who remembers?"
"But you remember The Shadow."
"I am The Shadow."

She felt him watching her as she ordered the clams and another gin and tonic. She pictured a heavy boulder rolling over a cliff, falling to the bottom of a canyon, cactus milk oozing from the trampled landscape.

She remembers forgetting to watch her step. She remembers forgetting to listen to the wind blow against the window. She remembers thinking, with this man, I can do this scene.

>The waiter said you two are somebody, aren't you?
>Ernest said without a doubt.
>Joan said of course.
>The waiter said I knew it!
>Joan said it's rude to ask if you don't remember.
>The waiter said I couldn't help it.
>Ernest said couldn't help forgetting?
>Joan said but we're so memorable.
>Ernest said who are we?
>Joan said I'm not sure.
>Ernest said that makes three of us.
>The waiter said you're comedians, right?
>Joan said we don't give autographs.
>Ernest said we cherish our privacy.
>The waiter said I won't tell anyone you're here.
>Joan said who are we?
>Ernest said you decide.
>Joan said to the waiter it's a secret.
>Ernest said to him I'll give you a hint. Get lost.

She remembers the details. The candle inside a red glass bowl. The waiter's red hair. The pimentos Ernest removed from his martini olives with one of her paper umbrellas. The sunburned look of her hands against the white tablecloth. The *we* they used when they spoke to the waiter. But she will not let her memory turn these details into valentines.

>She said, "I don't want to leave until the wind stops."
>"It's too late to chicken out."
>"Don't you ever hole up?"
>"Always," he told her.

Joan remembers their bowed heads as they walked into the night-time Santa Ana wind. Their flapping clothes. She hugged her briefcase against her chest. His hands were in his pockets. The air was filled with dust and smoke. The cameramen were rushing toward the hills, where a fire had started that would later be described as spectacular. She could not hear her heels tap the sidewalk. She heard sirens instead. She had no idea where they were going. But they were together, stride for stride.

*   *   *

    Once, when Joan stayed up late to work, to go through invoices, to go through the motions in order not to go to bed, her husband had called out for her. This was something he had never done.
    She turned off the light in the den and did not walk slowly down the dark hallway to their bedroom. She was worried that something old and unspeakable had made him call out that way. But when she reached him, there seemed to be nothing wrong. He was having trouble sleeping, that was all.
    He asked her to lie down next to him, offered to give her a back rub. Joan did not say, "What's gotten into you?" She let his hands work her shoulders and her neck, let his thumbs move in waves up and over her spine, there in the dark, gently pushing her edginess to the tips of her nerves and beyond, out, free, as if he knew what he were doing, as if he had done this sort of thing before, as if this were not the first time. And she thought: someone has shown you how to do this, you have done this with someone else. This was his way of telling her. This was his way of asking her to take it. Which is what she did. She said, "Thank you. This is good."
    She heard him laugh, but assumed that she was mistaken, that he had simply smiled out loud at his giving her something she needed, something good. So good that she did not wonder at first what was happening when she felt his knees pressed too hard against the back of her forearms, and his buttocks atop her buttocks, his hands kneading her neck and her shoulders in that good, knowing way, but then suddenly just pushing. Pushing her face into the pillow, holding her head down so that she couldn't breathe, so that she found herself kicking the heels of her feet against his broad back, and still she couldn't breathe—she hadn't thought to take a deep breath, why should she?—and then she couldn't think, couldn't fight.
    When he released her and rolled off, this time unmistakably laughing, he said, "It was just a joke, for crying out loud. I was only joking. Who do you think I am, anyway?"

*   *   *

Pillow Talk

"I'm not going to ask you what's wrong, Joanie. I already did that."
"Nothing's wrong. Let's be normal."
"And you already used that answer. I know when you're trying to jerk me around."
"Not always."
"But I'm prepared to enjoy it. Are you enjoying it?"
"I called because this is what normal people do when they're apart."
"Normal people never say 'let's be normal.' Where are you?"
"I'm in the den."
"Of course."
"It's cozy, Ernest."
"It's not cozy. It's tight. We should dig you a hole in the backyard. What are you wearing?"
"A blue nightgown."
"Go into the kitchen, Joanie. I want to picture my wife in her royal blue nightgown in the big kitchen of our big house in the desert."
"It's just blue. Not royal. Why are you calling me 'Joanie'?"
"This is how we talk in Houston about the wives. The guy from Texas A&M has a Mitzie. The one from MIT has a Clementine he calls Clemie. We talk about our big houses and the wives. Mine dwells in the den."
"I don't dwell."
"She's a coyote."
"You wish."
"A lone wolf."
"You're the wolf, Ernest."
"We like that about me."
"If I asked you if you were alone, you'd probably say 'yes.'"

"Probably."

"Because you want to keep me guessing."

"I want you to have a good time. Which comes down to the same thing."

"In your book."

"According to which, you now go into the kitchen. Didn't I give you a royal blue nightgown?"

"I'll put it on."

"Atta girl!"

Joan goes into the bedroom to change into the nightgown that she never wears, that was designed for a voluptuous, statuesque woman, and that makes her wonder what Ernest sees when he sees her. Perhaps he intended with this gift for her to play dress-up: put on the grown-up clothes, then wiggle her fanny and bat her eyelashes.

As she reaches her arms through the blousey sleeves, her hands brush against one of the exposed beams that decorate the low ceiling. It is not the den that's tight, she thinks—it's this room, with its old-world dressers and night tables, its looming beams, heavier and darker than railroad ties, like some medieval theater, where mortification takes place.

"Are you in the kitchen? Give me the details."

"I'm sitting at the breakfast counter, where the phone is. In the nightgown you gave me. I don't know why I'm cooperating."

"It's better that way, that you don't know."

"I'm aware of that."

"What else are you aware of?"

"The mosaic in the center of the kitchen floor. It scares me a little."

"It's supposed to. It's Spanish. Did you turn a light on?"

"No. I don't want anyone to know I'm alone here."

"Nobody can see the house from the street."

"They can see it from the other side, where the hedge is not so tall. They can see it from the desert. Which tonight seems even more like the desert. Why are you laughing?"

"Because you're funny. You don't mean to be, but you are. What are you drinking?"

"Gin and tonic."

"Are your legs crossed?"

"How do you want them to be, Ernest?"

"I want them to be slightly apart. I want your bare feet resting casually on the second rung of the barstool."

"This isn't like you."

"Tomorrow morning I'm going to be able to tell the guys that you're putty in my hands."

"Even though I'm not."

"I'm up for the challenge. I taste victory."

"Say whatever you like."

"I will. You'd hate this hotel, Joanie. It claims to have the biggest swimming pool in the world. Tell me how the renovations are going."

"They've finished laying the tiles. The workmen take their shoes and socks off before they come inside. They say their shoes make the whole place echo. They say the echoes are *amenazante*. But I think they take their shoes and socks off because it feels good, the cold tiles underfoot, beautiful and chilly."

"Like you."

"This house reminds me of one of the old California missions. The woodwork is so heavy, dark—"

"Like me."

"Are we even?"

"The way I figure it, Joanie, that'll never happen."

"I'm not up to sparring with you."

"Yes you are. Otherwise you'd tell me what's going on, and why you called."

"I'd like us to have a normal conversation, that's all."

"We should stick with what we're good at."

"What are you finding there, for example, in the ground?"

"We're finding too much water too close to the surface. The whole place is sinking. But when we put things into centimeters and geological time, nobody wants to listen. So they're going to build more skyscrapers downtown and forget about it. I'll be home in three days. What are you doing?"

"I'm replenishing."

"I should have known."

"What is she drinking? The woman you're with?"

"Gin and tonic."

Ernest seems to have something new in mind, a phone game whose rules they will make up along the way. Like the possibility of a third player. Like the winner thinking he has won before the game gets underway.

Joan could put an end to it. This is what she believes, even though her legs are slightly apart, and her bare feet are resting casually on the second rung of the barstool. Even though she sees herself giving in to the luxury of mindlessness. But she could put an end to it. She could hang up. Or she could tell him about the girl who came to the house after dark, on the day he left for Houston. Not a girl, as it turned out, though Joan thinks of her as a girl, but a young woman as petite and scrawny as Joan herself. She could have been Joan's sister, they looked so much alike. But the young woman's blond hair was long and parted in the middle, hippie style, and her jewelry was gauche, and she spoke in a sluttish and crudely matter-of-fact manner—the way Ernest, perhaps, hoped Joan would speak when she put on the royal blue nightgown.

"What is your room like? In that hotel?"
"Big enough for a small rodeo. I'm lying on the extra-large king size bed with a bourbon on the rocks. A manly drink. My legs are slightly apart."
"You don't sound like you."
"Ask me if I have any clothes on, Joanie."
"You sound like somebody else. Do you have any clothes on?"
"Just socks and underwear. I'm wiggling my toes at you, sending chills up and down your thorny spine. I'm a sexual magnet."
"You seem to think I want to play."
"Of course you do. How about if I put the balls in your court?"
"You'd like that. I'll just lie here and hold the bat."
"You're mixing your metaphors."
"Ball one. High and outside pedantry. You can do better than that, toots."
"Toots? You're in an awfully good mood."
"I'm in Texas."
"I don't ever want to go there."
"I've seen you in a good mood, Joanie. More than once. I'd swear to it in a court of law."
"You also swore you'd never go to Texas."
"Not in court. Not with my hand on the Bible."
"At the time, you were serious."
"At the time, I was in serious mourning. I wanted revenge. Then it died down. But I'll never step foot in Dallas."
"People do things they say they'll never do."
"And we're thankful for that."
"I'm not thankful, Ernest."

"Don't kid yourself."

"It's not like you to call yourself a sexual magnet. A sexual anything. You don't talk like that."

"I'm breaking new ground. Keeping up with the times. Calling a spade a spade."

"Maybe I'm talking to someone else."

"Maybe I'm always someone else."

"I think I'll go put on a sweater."

"We'll wait for your return with baited breath. That's 'baited', Joanie, with an 'i'."

Joan moves through the house in the dark, hearing the menacing echo of her husband's laughter, that devilish low chuckle, the pleasure he takes in improvising, keeping her on edge, winding himself up. She opens the deepest drawer of his dresser, puts on his bulky red sweater. Even so, she cannot get rid of the chill—it's as if the nighttime desert air lodged itself in her skin from the moment she opened the front door and let that girl inside who asked for help, who had burns on her arms and on her face. Beat up and burned and asking for help, but not tearful, as Joan imagined her sister would have been tearful, if she had a sister.

She had not been frightened by the girl's wounds, not afraid to look, to tend them with ointments and ice, to listen as the girl told everything that happened. What frightened Joan was that they looked so much alike and the girl wasn't crying but telling her story with a smug sort of enthusiasm, as if it confirmed some prediction, as if it were the oldest story in the book.

"I'm back."

"Look, Joanie. You said nothing's wrong, right?"

"Right."

"And we both know that we live in dangerous times. Are you following me? Earthquakes, firebombs, men on towers with guns. This could be our last conversation."

"So let's talk like an ordinary couple."

"I had something else in mind. I'm taking off my socks."

"Maybe we should get a dog. A big one, Ernest. A collie. A well-trained dog who could protect us. And she could lie here on the kitchen floor and shed all over the screaming birds in this mosaic. We could talk about her over the phone."

"Lassie."

"Exactly."

"I'd rather leave it up to you to protect us."

"I don't think I can."

"That's my point. Lassie is too sure of herself. She's a cocky bitch. A know-it-all. Those birds are singing, by the way, not screaming. They're supposed to remind you of angels."

"Then they're the ones who were kicked out of Heaven."

"Lucky them. Tell me about the patio and the fig trees and the blooming hibiscus. I'll consider it foreplay."

"With you, Ernest, everything is foreplay."

"Lucky me."

"That depends on what you think I meant."

"I'm disregarding all meanings that might be unflattering."

"Your timing is way off."

"I don't think so. I think you're wavering. I think you want me to have my way with you. I think you're about to succumb. Repeat after me, slowly, succumb."

"I don't want to be toyed with."

"Whatever you say. You're the boss."

"I sometimes wish that were true."

"But mainly you like it the way it is. If the house didn't remind you of a mission—"

"That's not it."

"Convince me. Say something uninhibited."

"I've never been a prude. You know that."

"You've been a Catholic."

"That was a long time ago."

Joan remembers the day she went with her classmates to the mission in Carmel where Father Serra is buried. She was sent back inside at the end of the day to look for Sister Dolores, one of the oldest of her teachers, who almost never spoke outside the classroom and to whom the young Joan had been fearfully devoted. She found them in a candlelit corner, kneeling, their arms around each other—Sister Dolores and another nun who lived there at the mission, who said to Joan that she was the flesh and blood sister of Sister Dolores. And Joan could see the family resemblance, both bodies a kind of bosomy fortress, both faces accustomed to conviction. Joan wanted to be a nun then, one of them, just like them, with that same, sure look on her face. But when she expressed this desire at home, fervent and convinced, it was decided that she would go to public school from then on.

She is thinking that if she had become a nun, the battered girl would have taken her story someplace else. She would have been too shy, too respectful to tell an immaculate bride of Christ about the two men who took her into the desert and held her down, then forced her mouth open and jacked off into her mouth—that's how the girl told it—the younger man first, who tasted like piss, then the older one whose eyes were watering, both of them talking about each other's hard-ons and making jokes.

"I know when you're holding out on me, Joanie."

"Do you intend to call me that all evening?"

"I intend for you to give in. We're going to do something new here. Over the phone. You're going to let that nightgown slip off your shoulders. I'll stay on the phone as long as it takes."

"I'm not a pushover."

"Surprise me. Become one. Just for the time being. We could make this a quickie, but if I were you, I'd be extravagant."

"I usually am."

"I know. I admire it. I admire my luck in falling for a tight-lipped blond with considerable assets. I admire this enormous hotel and our exclusive neighborhood in Palm Springs and the chance to forget what it was like to be among the Harvard boys on a need-based scholarship."

"You don't forget anything, Ernest. Ever."

"True."

"That's not that funny."

"Yes it is."

"If I were a Mitzie or a Clemie, we wouldn't be doing this. I'd have my legs crossed, my bare feet would not be resting casually on the second rung of the barstool. We'd be talking about our dog."

"And you'd be drinking a strawberry daiquiri instead of gin with a splash of tonic. The only contact you'd have with missions is the missionary position. And you wouldn't be wondering whether your hairy-chested husband has removed his underwear."

"I wasn't wondering."

"You were hoping. Visualizing."

"Do you think I'm trying to tease you?"

"You don't have to try. You're a natural. A pro. World class. You're forcing me to take them off."

"No, I'm definitely not."

"You leave me no choice, Joanie. The monster has risen from the deep. He must come up for air. He must have breathing room. You have beckoned and he answers your call."

"I didn't beckon."

"He lurches westward, hapless creature, toward his mate so far away."

"Stop it, Ernest."

"I can stop the poeticizing. As for the rest—"

"I think we should say goodnight."

"So you can go sit in that mortuary of a den and drink your gin?"

"Yes."

"Nothing doing. You're not going anywhere."

When they got back from the hospital, Joan let the girl take a bath, and insisted that she spend the night. Joan made them both a drink. They sat in the den, where the girl told Joan that she didn't fight, didn't struggle when the men held her down and put their cocks in her mouth and burned her arms and face and tits with cigarettes, burned the hair off her goddamned hippie cunt—that's what they called it. The younger one wanted to shove a piece of cactus up inside her, but the older one said burning was the thing to do, she's a heretic sure as shit. Then the younger one couldn't stop laughing. Barbie-que, whoop-de-doo.

The girl said it would have been even worse if she hadn't gone blank as blank and pretended that she had no body, that she was something else altogether—a cloud, a breeze. In a way, the girl said, I guess I overpowered the mother-fuckers.

"You can't force me to stay on the phone, Ernest."

"Correct. My needs are at your mercy."

"And what you mean by your needs, I take it, is pillow talk over the phone."

"If you can manage it."

"We don't do pillow talk at home. We don't say anything."

"Take this as a golden opportunity. I acknowledge your limited experience, but offer you the leading role nonetheless."

"You want me to talk about putting my hands on you, my mouth."

"Begin at the ankles and slowly work your way up."

"I should have called somebody else. A girlfriend."
"You don't have any girlfriends."
"I have the women who work at the shop."
"You're the owner, the head honcho. They're not your friends."
"You don't know everything."
"Tell you what. When I get home we'll have a pajama party. We'll give each other manicures and play Monopoly. We'll drink rum and coke and stay up all night."
"I don't need you to be my girlfriend, Ernest."
"Yes you do."

Joan glides to the refrigerator for more ice. She has to admit that she called her husband because she knew that he would chide her, toughen her up. Someone else, one of the women who worked for her at the dress shop, might have agreed that the desert is too quiet, that people need protection. And in her present—she would say unaccountable—state, Joan might have spoken about the girl, about the uncanny resemblance, about the two men and their hard-ons and their jokes, about the oldest story in the book. Someone else might possibly have lured Joan into speaking of these things, and more. She might have been lured into weeping about the nothing that sometimes felt like everything.

Joan wipes the tears from her face, backhanded, harsh, and tells herself that she is grateful for her husband's wanting things to go his way, his needing her to pull herself together, to play it out.

"Is it true that you have no clothes on?"
"Buck naked except for my watch."
"Take it off. And turn off the lights."
"You're not going to make me vow that I'm alone?"
"No. Either way."
"Atta girl, Joanie!"
"Rub some of that bourbon on you, then put your drink down."
"I detect some genuine aggressiveness. Some team spirit."
"Are you lying on your back or on your stomach?"
"How do you want me?"
"Back."
"I'm all yours. Be gentle."
"I enter your room in that nightgown."

"The one you're wearing."

"Royal blue."

"Which you did put on, right? You said so. You put me on hold while you went to change."

"Yes. The one I'm supposed to be wearing while I sit in our big kitchen. So you can tell the guys—"

"Where you are, in fact, sitting?"

"You're spoiling the scene, Ernest. I was about to enter your hotel room."

"You're diddling with me, Joanie. Where, in fact, are you?"

"I'm about to be with you, next to, beneath, on top of."

"You gave me the distinct impression that you were cooperating. For all I know, you could be sitting in the den, wearing a pants suit, sticking it to me."

"I'm wearing the nightgown, Ernest. I'm in the kitchen. My legs are slightly apart, et cetera."

"You're playing ball."

"Yes."

"You're a willing participant."

"We're partners in crime."

"I like the sound of that."

"I thought you might."

"It would be a crime to let this baby go to waste."

"We won't let that happen."

"I knew I could count on you, Joanie."

Joan sits huddled and cold in the dark kitchen. She finishes her drink and then whispers into the phone a story about a mysterious woman who appears at Ernest's bedside, out of nowhere, like a breeze or a cloud, a voluptuous annunciation in royal blue whose very breath is smoke, who blows a sweet hot desert smoke into his ears and across his lips and around his balls, who enflames and ravishes him, and whose face he never sees.

* * *

They came, eventually, to have a persistent companion, a young man, younger by a decade than they were, and the sort of talker who couldn't help himself, who couldn't stop. They didn't say so, but he was a godsend.

Once, and only once, he found Joan alone when he dropped in unannounced at the cocktail hour, as had become his custom. Ernest, it turned out, was out of town on business. It was wintertime in the desert, absolutely still, almost too clear. Half-wishing he hadn't shown up, Joan suggested that they drive out to one of the local hotsprings. They would take their drinks with them, watch the sunset, and feel the chill come on. He would try, because she asked him, as a special favor, not to talk too much.

But when they were settled side-by-side at the edge of the steamy brown water, it was Joan who found herself wanting to break the silence, without knowing what she would speak, or why, knowing that in any case she would not get sentimental and girlish. Not even on an evening like that one, when it was cold enough to keep remembering from becoming indolent and dreamy; cold enough that she might gather her ghosts and speak their eulogies, speak her own, speak without resorting to any of the words whose faces made her afraid—like "sorrow," like "beloved," like "mother," like "help me."

As far as she was concerned, she spoke only a matter-of-fact point. "You're a good friend. Especially for him. He needs you." She pulled her collar up and sipped her drink. In the twilight they watched the steam rise off the water, eerie and seductive. Be with me, the heavy mist seemed to say. Be like me. Be something and nothing at the same time.

Finally he said, "The way I figure it, Ernest needs me in order to have somebody to tell one of these days that he needs *you*." She shook her head, thinking no, that is not it at all. "In any case," she told him, "you can be sure that it is not any particular need that I need you for." She laughed, and elbowed him to get him to do the same, but he was silent.

* * *

I've Got You under My Skin

There were no lights on in the bedroom. Ernest was buttoning his shirt. Joan was still in bed, watching her husband dress.

Ernest said, "Do you remember that you told me that I became a geologist because I was made of stone?"

"No."

"Yes you do." Ernest rubbed it in. "We were in the mountains. Just before we were married."

Joan could have said that she had meant something else, something about Ernest's hard "thing." But instead she said, "I don't remember. I don't believe I said that." She watched him pack a change of clothes.

"You look like a tortoise," he told her.

"Your favorite animal." Joan pulled the sheets up over her head.

Ernest approached the bed and lifted the sheet. "*You're* my favorite animal," he said. He returned to his packing. "You'll need to leave by ten," he added.

"Yes," said Joan. "Timing is everything."

"I never said that."

Joan uncovered her face. "I'm only agreeing with you," she explained. "I'm being agreeable."

"I never said timing was everything."

Neither of them spoke for a while. Then Ernest was ready to go. "Are you taking Carol with you?" he asked.

"I'd rather take Vince."

"Vince is mine." Ernest looked at his wife. They half-smiled at each other in the dark.

"I'll get there on time," said Joan.

"Enough said."

"More than enough. Go fishing."

"I'm going."

The two men were sitting on rocks at the bank of a stream, gutting fish. Ernest was not thinking about where Joan was going. He did not want to imagine the place. He wanted to listen to Vince talk.

Between them lay thirteen rainbow trout, a good catch. They had thrown back everything under eight inches. "Inches have meaning," Ernest had said.

"What I like about fishing up here," Vince was saying, "is that nobody else does it. No campers, no card-players, no girls in cut-offs. They all go to the lakes. Arrowhead. Big Bear. A stream trout doesn't occur to them. Nixon's silent majority on their boats on a lake. Think of the noise level, the shriekers, the pollution from the point of view of the grassy bottom. What I'm saying is, give me a stream, a running brook. Never mind your line gets caught in the trees, the constant entanglements. This is nature."

"Men in the woods," said Ernest.

"Right on. You know what I like about these fish? You're not gonna guess, so I'll tell you. I like that you can't tell them apart. Not until you start cleaning them. You catch them, you pull them out, you take a look, and you say, they all look alike. Check this one out." Vince selected a trout from the pile and held it the way Ernest showed him, not by the body but by the gills. "Male or female?"

Ernest looked at the fish.

"Can't tell, right? Not until you open her up." Vince cut through the tough underside of the trout.

"And even then—" said Ernest.

"And even then, without the eggs inside, who knows? You'd have to call in some fish scientist, some guy with expertise in the animal subtleties, the spots of color that say jack to the untrained eye. Let's face it, geology in this matter is worthless. You can show me rocks, point out the layers, provide the time frames, but males and females don't figure into it—"

"I don't have to think about it."

"And I can show you trees—but again, no male to female gradations come into play. Except to your poets. To them, all trees are dicks, i.e. male. But take birds. Birds are easy. You look at birds and you see the men have the color. No problem. Mockingbirds are tricky, I'll give them that. But these fish—"

"They all look alike on the outside."

"We should be so lucky," said Vince. "Look. Eggs. This one's a dame."

"There ain't nothing like one."

"Nothin' you can name."

"That is anything like a dame."

Ernest scooped a fingerful of the milky eggs from the open belly of the trout and put the finger in his mouth.

"I couldn't do that," said Vince. "Man oh man, no way. Bad enough we have to clean her out. Go ahead. Call me a pussy. I'm still not doing it. What does it taste like?"

Ernest looked at Vince and grinned. "A female," he said.

Joan was doing the driving. This was her territory, Palm Springs to Enseñada, the desert. She was thinking about Ernest, about the arduous sincerity of their first lovemaking, about getting it over with.

She was wearing a long denim skirt, a red peasant blouse, and her largest pair of sunglasses. With a red and white bandanna she had tied her hair into a short ponytail. She looked as if she were heading south of the border in order to shop.

Carol was wearing a sundress that displayed cleavage. This was her first trip to Mexico. In the back seat were Joan's overnight bag and Carol's suitcase. Joan planned on staying one night. Carol prepared for unpredictable changes in the weather. The two women had been on the road for over an hour, listening to the radio, saying nothing.

They had become friends because Ernest and Vince had become friends. And then Vince and Joan, sort of. Vince worked for the National Forest Service, a tribute, he called it, to the sixties—an outdoors job, a brown uniform, low pay. He and Ernest met on San Jacinto mountain. Joan and Carol met in Joan's kitchen. Carol brought potato salad and introduced herself as a woman poet.

Joan was remembering the surprising feel of Ernest's weight, the thick redundancies, the camouflaging densities that had mattered then and still did.

Carol turned off the radio and lit a cigarette. "Does Ernest ever say things to you while you're doing it?"

"No."

"Nothing?"

"Nothing."

"Vince talks the whole time. I'm not kidding."

Joan knew that, under the circumstances, Carol would demand little of her, would sit in silence the whole way if that's what Joan wanted. Joan knew that, if she wanted to, she could behave badly and get away with it.

So she said, "Tell me."

"What Vince says?"
"Yes."

Ernest and Vince found a cool spot in the woods to eat lunch and wait for late afternoon to come around, when the fishing would again be worth it.

Vince bit into his sandwich and said, "I caught Carol last week in the bathroom touching her breasts. Said her doctor told her to do it. Feel yourself up, doctor's orders. Carol said she was just checking for problems, bumps, what the hell do I know. She was standing in front of the mirror with her arm up. Pressing around with the tips of her fingers, like this." Vince demonstrated the procedure. "Which was bad enough. Think about it. But can we leave it at that? No. We have to have this booklet open on the counter, like a medical booklet with medical pictures. What the basic tit really looks like on the inside. This is what I have to encounter out of the blue. The woman I live with poking herself and looking at those pictures like they were nothing."

Ernest imitated Vince's demonstration, felt himself up. "I don't feel anything, no bumps," he said.

Vince laughed and shook his head. "I'm glad I don't have tits," he said. "They used to be one of the things in life I could relate to. All kinds: little cones, medium peaches, big in terms of a handful, not to mention biggest, boobs, knockers, jugs, headlights, the whole gauntlet. Call me a romantic. The body shape of them is what I'm talking about. The form, the classicism. I have that sort of eye, for forms, an artistic eye."

"Carol's are about right."

"On the outside she's got a pair I'd be proud to call my own."

"Me too."

"But consider the pictures. I don't think I can see a woman's breasts artistically anymore. They've fallen out of the form category. Now my eye sees tissue, fat, blood. Who needs it?"

"Not me," said Ernest.

"Think about it. Those pictures—"

"Forget the insides," said Ernest. "It's all shit."

Joan's mother had been a believer in spilling your guts. That's what women were *for*, she would say. And she would say, "Look at the statistics." Joan was asking for it. You're asking for cancer, she said to Joan before she died. You should try to behave like a normal woman, and *talk*.

Joan was thinking that Carol should have been her mother's daughter. Carol thought that the death of Louise Bogan warranted a public display of mourning at Joan's dress shop on Palm Canyon Drive, in front of the customers, while Joan was working. Carol was going to tell Joan what Vince said while they were doing it.

"You're not going to believe me," said Carol.

"Try me."

"I mean, like you and I haven't known each other that long. But then again, with women, the intimacy thing can be instantaneous, don't you think? I don't know. I can't believe I brought this up. Are you sure?"

"Yes," said Joan.

"This is unbelievable. Okay. No wait. Like this is what Vince says—he says his dick really found itself around 1964. That's when it got politics, he says, when it blossomed into a political animal, became a news junky, learned the words to all the songs, I swear to god. He calls my clit Clio, muse of history, can you believe it? So wait, I'll be like getting ready for bed, right? and Vince, he'll start singing "Aquarius" or something, but it's not him singing—it's his *dick*! Swear to god. It's gotta be some sort of ventriloquism, what else could it be? But it's the *dick* coming on to me with this singing! And that's only the warm-up. Then it goes into a talking voice, picks a year, say like 1969, and starts reviewing the headline events of that year, talking non-stop, coming at me the whole time with Sirhan Sirhan is tried and convicted, the gall or what's his name resigns as president of France, *The Godfather* sells, I don't know, a zillion copies, on and on, in and out. Chappaquid*dick*, it says. It's unbelievable. Like when it's gearing up for the news, doing that number from *Easy Rider*—"*Lookin' for adventure, or whatever comes my way*"—already I'm a puddle of juice. Is this embarrassing you or anything?"

"No."

"It's gone over the same stuff so many times: I mean, like riots in Cleveland, Detroit, Newark, Watts, the death of Woody Guthrie, the marches, the assassinations, the moon landing, Vietnam, on and on, like re-runs of Walter Cronkite, in fact it sounds sort of like Walter Cronkite, it's got a deeper voice than Vince does, slower, older, like it's had pronouncing lessons. The broadcaster, he calls it, the disseminator, and he's like completely serious. Last night the dick started out by singing "Hey, Jude," you know, kind of swaying back and forth, coming at me—*then go and get her-er-er*—it's one of my favorite numbers, Vince's lips are barely moving, but the dick is singing its heart out. I can't tell you what this is really like, it's incredible, you'll have to take my word for it. God, just telling you about this is making me horny."

Joan did not expect this. She would have known what to do with a string of obscene endearments, or erotic fantasizing. But the news? But singing? She did not know what to do with this. She did not know how to keep herself from smiling.

"It's hysterical, isn't it?" Carol went on. "Unbelievable. You're not going to say anything, right? Vince would kill me. No, in fact, he wouldn't. But try not to say anything anyway."

"I'll try."

"I can't believe Ernest doesn't say a word. You mean like zero? Nada? Neither one of you?"

Joan imagined herself telling Carol about the occasional background music, her husband's mating call, the Sinatra record that he would put on: Sinatra telling himself to use his mentality, wake up to reality. And then, after the thing had been accomplished, the expressions on their faces that had something to do with the music and something to do with the words that did not pass between them.

"It's fine," she told Carol. "It's what we want. It's just the way we want it."

Vince was playing his guitar, singing his lugubrious rendition of "Hang Down Your Head, Tom Dooley," while Ernest did the cooking. Ernest was wearing a red apron tied at the waist. He liked cooking this way, the grill balanced on rocks that encircled the fire, heavy skillets, thick slices of potato and onion. His campfire was perfect. Ernest had serious respect for campfires, barbecues, controlled combustion—had it, he claimed, from day one.

A few campers who did not fish the streams smelled Ernest's cooking and came over to have a look and talk inches. One man said his wife almost died from touching a sick fish.

"Had to be something else," said Ernest.

"She was sick for a month," said the man. He had a low-slung heavy belly. "Couldn't get out of bed. That your wife's apron? I gave mine one like that, red, for Christmas, that I've never seen her wear."

"Keeps the grease out of my crotch," said Ernest.

The man looked at Vince and then at Ernest, as if he were checking his bearings. Then he said, "I'm fundamentally sure it was touching a fish that made her sicker than a dog. My boy, he found it, washed up on the lakeshore, came and put it into her hands. So she had to touch it. Didn't do nothing to him, but it made her sick, I'm telling you. A month of it I had to live with. Me and my boy."

"Your boy," said Vince. "He didn't get sick?"

"I just said so. Am I talking to myself here? May as well go back to my camp, where she's at."

Vince looked at the man. Ernest didn't.

"Sorry," Vince told him.

"My wife says it's a woman thing. Something women get from touching sick fish."

"A wives' tale," said Ernest.

"Maybe so," said the man. "Your wife ever been sick?"

Ernest said nothing.

"I know what it's like," Vince told the man. "I know what you're saying. I've been there."

"Good," said the man.

He watched Ernest slice a lemon into neat wedges, remove the seeds, and then sprinkle lemon juice over the frying trout. "Mine cried all the time. That's how sick."

"That's the worst," said Vince. "That's when you have to face the dividing line between us and them. Maybe you sensed it all along. But it's not until they start in on the serious crying that the difference really sinks its teeth into you."

"You feel all alone when they do that," said the man.

"Like an island," Vince agreed. "Like the only tree in the forest. Like nothing. This is what we're saying. A man crying isn't the same thing."

"It's tragic," said Ernest.

"Breathtaking," said Vince.

"Yeah," said the man.

Joan referred to the place as the doctor's office.

She and Carol were in their hotel room in Enseñada. Carol unpacked while Joan opened the curtains and the windows, took in the ocean view, limp waves cradling nothing.

Joan said, "I have to go to the doctor's office now. I'll meet you here at the patio bar between five and six."

The doctor's office was in the center of town, on the second floor above a store that specialized in leather. Not the cheap stuff. Joan smelled good leather jackets and skirts and saddles. She took the thick smell with her to the back of the store, up the narrow stairs, and into a small gray room furnished with a wooden table and chair, an electric fan, and a wide metal shelf. There was no window there. There were two women in the room. There was no doctor. The old one, the midwife, seemed to Joan to belong to the center of the earth, to a prehistoric silence. The other woman was young and beautiful. She counted Joan's American dollars, set Joan's clothes neatly over the back of the chair, led her to the wide metal shelf, held her hand, whispered Hail Marys, *llena eres de gracia*, over and over. The young woman had beautiful black eyes and hair. Joan thought, what a good daughter she would make. She thought, I would like her to live in my house, I would like to buy her things, I would like to take her picture standing next to Ernest, smiling.

Joan did not think about the pain. The silent midwife was careful. Joan would be all right. The beautiful young woman said, *Sí, bueno.* They let her lie on the metal shelf for a while, afterwards, bleeding but not hurt, smelling leather. Joan had remembered to bring a sanitary napkin. It was in her purse. The beautiful young woman took the sanitary napkin out of Joan's purse and did not take anything else. After a while she said to Joan that her time was up, that it was time for the next señora.

Before she left the building, Joan bought leather vests for Ernest and Vince, a handbag for Carol, and a fine pair of high-heeled boots for herself. Then she drove back to the hotel, showered, got a fresh sanitary napkin from her overnight bag, put her clothes back on, breathed into the package that contained her purchases, and headed for the hotel bar. *Llena de gracia*? No.

Ernest and Vince watched the man with the belly walk back to his camp.

"He thinks you're married," said Ernest.

"He thinks you're a fruit," said Vince.

"I am." Ernest cupped his hand over his aproned crotch. "A banana."

"Seriously. Think about it. He's gonna go back and tell them about your apron and your lemon slices. The daintiness with which you prepare our meal. Visualize the implications. On the other hand, do we care? I say we don't. At least the man has something to talk about. Do we want to deny him something to say to his wife?"

"Maybe we should kiss."

"Now you're talking. A significant conversation piece. A piece of news. I can see you know what I'm getting at. People have to have something to say to each other. They'll talk about anything."

"Sick wives," said Ernest.

"Sickness of any sort on anybody, you're right. Did you notice that guy looked pregnant? Now there's a what-if for you. Pregnant men. Guys with birth canals, ovaries, the works. It's a question of engineering, higher mathematics probably, in order to make room for everything. I'm not talking about this sex change stuff, where it's gotta be one way or the other, same old story, yin or yang. I'm saying, what if everybody gets the whole enchilada? So a guy checks into the hospital, has the baby, goes home, and then lays down with the naked wife and dips his wick. Likewise for the women."

"A democracy of organs."

"You got it. Like what? Like worms. They can go either way, ac or dc. Imagine it. We advance to the worm stage. But here's the crucial question. What difference does it make? Do we acquire world peace? Let's say that guy over there gives birth. So what? So what follows is the fashion industry makes the appropriate seasonal adjustments. There's new products everywhere you look. Corporate America goes on maternity leave. Steel-workers vote for breast-feeding in the lunchrooms. But is there a wrenching change in our outlook? Call me a skeptic, but I don't think so."

"So would you do it?"

"Give birth? Good question. This is what it comes down to. The particular instance. The personal choice, yes or no. You start at square *numero uno*: this is America, where every freakin' man faces a decision like a man."

"God bless America," Ernest said.

"Right on. So here's our hypothetical situation—Carol gets me pregnant. What do I do?"

Vince gave this some thought while Ernest dished up the food. "You consider all the factors," said Ernest. "The individual circumstances, the timing. You look at what you can handle. At what you need, from the other person. And what you don't need—that's what Joan's doing in Ensenada. She got an address and went down there. I thought Carol might have told you."

Vince took off his cap and rubbed his head. "She's having an operation? Getting rid of a—?"

"No," Ernest interrupted. "Not getting rid. Just not having."

"Geezus, man. I didn't know. I've been shooting my mouth off."

"Don't stop."

"I'm stopping."

"I mean it."

Vince looked at Ernest. "All right, let's face it. Maybe the arrival of this topic was inevitable. Maybe I was made to bring it up so you could have an opening."

"I don't want an opening."

"Maybe it's not evident that as a listener I have qualities. I do. I know the deep woods from listening. So lay it on me."

Ernest hugged his knees and looked at the fire.

In the lobby of the hotel Joan looked in the mirror, reapplied her lipstick, and imagined herself walking among ruins in some warm place. Ernest was there too, but she could not see him.

She found Carol on the patio, drinking a margarita, talking with the waiter. Joan sat down and ordered two shots of tequila. She made a point of watching the waiter walk away.

Carol said, "I don't know what to say."

Joan elbowed her companion, chummed it up. "So what's with you and the waiter?"

"Are you all right?"

"Sí, bueno," said Joan. She took off her sunglasses, as if to offer proof.

Carol smiled and finished her drink. "He likes women," she said. "The waiter. I mean really likes them, you know what I mean? In a respectful way that's hard to believe. I don't know how we got on the topic, but out he comes with this genuine appreciation of women in a sincere-sounding way that was a nice surprise, that's what I told him. How surprised I was to hear him say that, don't you think?"

"He's a dish," said Joan.

The waiter arrived with the tequila. Carol ordered another margarita. To Joan the waiter said, "La señora takes it straight."

Joan nodded and said, "Very."

The waiter bowed.

"See what I mean?" said Carol. "Did you see that bow? The respect? It's unbelievably hard for a woman to come across that kind of like open show of admiration. You know what I mean, how men are, the distrust thing, the mother thing, the whole male thing."

Joan drank a shot of tequila. "Are you sure?" she asked.

"You mean like, what is he really thinking? It's impossible to say. Me, I take things as they come. I see a bow and I think respect."

"You never know," said Joan. "About anything."

The waiter returned with Carol's drink. Both women gave him the once-over, openly gazed at his private bulges. They took their time. The waiter, red-faced, left the patio.

Carol leaned toward Joan and said, "We're acting like cunts."

"You mean like men."

Joan hoped that her smile didn't look as brittle as it felt.

Carol relaxed into a giggle. "You know," she said, "I swore to myself that if we talked about anything on the way down here it would be whatever you wanted. And did I hold up my end of the bargain? Of all the subject matter. The disseminator. It's unbelievable how my thoughts just come into my mouth, it's like I'm cursed with expressiveness. I guess that's what I get for being a poet."

They looked at the dingy ocean, the meager sunset. Then Carol went on. "I think there's like a reason Vince does his routine that goes way beyond political commitment. I mean, if the dick didn't sing its numbers and review the news, then what? Would we just be left lying there with nothing but the basic silence? I think he might be afraid of that."

"Aren't you?"

"Are you?"

"Yes."

"You're telling me a true feeling? In the sense of expressing a genuine inner fear?"

"Yes."

Carol reached for Joan's hand, but Joan made sure that the gesture turned into an awkward, seated high-five, of sorts.

"Do you want to tell me about this afternoon?"

"I bought you an extraordinary handbag," said Joan.

"Joan is deep," Ernest was saying. "Some women aren't, some are."

"Carol is deep," said Vince. "But not as deep as Joan."

"There's nothing wrong with shallow. A shallow woman can get the job done. With one like that you live, period."

"You live an everyday life," said Vince.

"But you never know with the deep ones." Ernest swept an arm toward the woods as if it evidenced his point. "There's a dangerous element. Anything can happen. The possibility of explosion—that's precisely the sort of thing that can keep a man vital. So of course, Joan and I, we decided, we're not ready to give that up."

Ernest looked at his watch. He took his plate and silverware into the cabin. He felt good about having said "Joan and I." The two of them, in this thing together. Joan and I, he repeated to himself. We're not ready to let everything get said and done, to clear the woods and put up a swing-set.

He returned to the campfire with a cold thermos and two coffee cups. "Martini time," he said. He was still wearing the red apron.

Vince heaped the last forkful of potato and onion into his mouth and said, "Would you refer to me in terms of being a deep person?"

"You're deep enough."

"The question is, though, the whole idea of deep. Like when you say deep enough, am I supposed to be happy about it?"

"Sure."

"I'm not as deep as you is what you're saying."

"I'm saying nobody needs special equipment to know what you're thinking. You vocalize. You've got the balance. The hard thing is to get the balance without getting soft. You've achieved this."

Vince nodded. "It takes constant work."

"Because you don't want to kiss the edge goodbye, say adios to control. That's the thing. Some people want this erosion. They give themselves over to pursuits, demands, luck, feelings. They lose control. They start fires somebody else has to put out. I've seen men do it. And of course women do it."

"But not Joan."

"She stays deep. Deep and hard." Ernest laughed.

"You're vocalizing," said Vince. "I've been noticing that. You, my man, are moving toward achieving the balance."

Ernest poured himself another drink. After a while he said, "Knowing the right time to crumble. That's the trick."

The four of them arrived at Joan and Ernest's house at the outskirts of town in time for Sunday cocktails. They unloaded the cars, then busied themselves—made drinks and hors d'oeuvres, rinsed trout, peeled potatoes. Ernest prepared the barbecue. The bustle was good, the banter. They used their mentality.

Joan said something obscenely clever about the waiter at the hotel in Ensenada. Ernest laughed out loud, too much. He had tears in his eyes. He couldn't stop. Carol joked that the last hysteric in the pool was a rotten egg. She and Ernest went for a swim.

Joan and Vince were left alone in the kitchen. They were the same height, both blond, too thin. He had fallen into the pool once and she had loaned him a pair of pants.

"You're wearing my pants," she told him.

"Forget the pants. They're not important."

"Why don't you keep them?"

"What's important is the here and now. I'm seeing you and it's hitting me, the whole thing, the circumstances, where you've been, an address in Ensenada provided by an unnamed acquaintance. I'm talking about seeing what it was like, like I was there. I think there was a woman on the premises."

"There were no so-called premises!" Joan snapped at him. This was not what she wanted to do, but he had drawn her out. Because he didn't know what he was saying. The premises. She took a deep breath. "You have some imagination," she told him.

"I can't help it," he said. "It's one of the things about me. Imagination, mainly visual. Like going to an unknown address—I'm seeing it, Joan. The room, the instruments, the look on your face. I see the whole thing. I feel it. That's what I'm saying."

"I don't want you to feel it, Vince."

"It can't be helped."

"Let it go. It has nothing to do with you."

"Talk to me." He started to reach for her.

"Stop it! Don't touch me! I can't—"

"Yes you can. Please."

Joan looked at Vince and tried to show him that she would not give in to the temptation to turn herself over to him. No matter what he offered. No matter how much she might want whatever he offered. She reminded herself that she had long since stopped believing in comfortings and condolences and reachings-out. Nothing could fix things, no one, not even Vince.

She got up and walked away from him, walked toward the pool.

And she thought about their arrival. She thought about how the two cars had pulled into the driveway almost simultaneously, and how the four of them had made wry remarks about the unlikelihood of such a convergence, of convergences in general, and how she had felt the nearness of Ernest's tense body, how she had told him that she was fine when he touched her lightly on the arm, just above the elbow, as if she were fragile, or as if he were.

* * *

One of the guys Ernest worked with—Howard, a good-looking guy, dark and lean, first rate earthquake man with a red bow-tie of a mouth from which a cigarette always dangled like an accessory, like an earring—this Howard announced one morning that he had finally found his future wife.

The guys were guests that day in a lab at Cal Tech, looking at the latest maps, and Howard said he was going to name one of the new fault lines after her, a small vein arching eastward from the deadly San Andreas. "Henceforth," he said, "this one here shall be known among us as Lola. May she be the death of me!"

They all approved of her name. None of them had ever known an actual Lola in person, but they could imagine one, they said, and she would be a gen-u-wine sex-pot.

Howard said amidst the whoops and the whistles, "Lest you have the wrong impression, my Lola is nobody's fool. Not a whit like most women, who we all know are anybody's fool." This made the others laugh the laugh they needed now and then, more often than not—it was the laugh that reminded them that men were men.

Then Howard went on about his Lola: "I can get all I want off her without any ga-ga. No music, no flowers, no candles, no bracelets, no I'm-gonna-die-without-you-baby." There was another burst of whoops and whistles.

Ernest was nodding. He was thinking about his own wife, who asked for no ga-ga, never had, and that was surely in her favor, even though she didn't put out on a regular basis. And he was thinking that Howard had made the right decision with this Lola—a good name, he was thinking, a name that made him want to meet her, to see for himself a Lola who could make a tail-chaser like Howard want to get married. But mainly he was thinking about his own wife, and he was thinking: I'm gonna die without you, baby. But it was only a thought.

* * *

I'm in the Mood for Love

Joan is in disguise. She has considered every detail, including a code-name. If asked—by a beach-combing busybody, for instance—she would say, with a pleasant smile, "My name is June, which rhymes with croon, swoon, and of course harpoon."

Joan is not, in fact, carrying any weapons. Her intention is simply to see the thing for herself—she means the thing that is going on between her husband and their friend Carol.

Ernest is incognito, but not very. He is easy to recognize. On the other hand, he is not concerned. He enjoys giving the impression that he has nothing to hide.

Lately he's been doing some weightlifting. He's planning on a flat stomach and lively pecs. Ernest has confidence in the plan—the way it keeps him focussed, the measurable results. He tells Carol that he has learned all the words to "My Baby Does the Hanky Panky."

Carol is wearing almost nothing. Her peach bikini is the same color as her skin. Carol thinks of everything she wears, or doesn't, as natural expressions of her role in life—which is to really be there for other people.

Carol gives Ernest's middle-aged belly a pat that is supposed to communicate reassurance and understanding. She is full of good intentions.

Joan understands "June" to be the sort of woman who would purchase an unbecoming, silly hat because even so small a frivolity makes her feel like part of something big—a big good time going on out there in the world. On a cruise ship, for example, like the *Love Boat*.

Joan is good at disguise. So good that she has not worn a costume since the Halloween in '49 when with terrifying success she passed herself off as a wounded GI. She has broken her long-standing no-more-costumes vow because she wants to know how serious it is, this thing between Carol and

Ernest, and what action to take, if action must be taken. She does not want to be left out of the picture, left alone, to fend for herself.

Ernest's accessories are the impulsive, celebratory result of the hard-on that developed as he was driving into Santa Monica for this afternoon at the beach. He has on mirrored sunglasses and an authentic cowboy hat—the get-up of a maverick, except for those loose-fitting red swim trunks that his wife bought for him a couple of years ago.

Ernest is pouring drinks from a frosty thermos—piña coladas, a rum punch, his favorite party drink since his father's funeral. Insofar as he thinks about it, Ernest thinks that he is having an affair with Carol because the opportunity to do so fell right into his lap. Literally.

Despite the clownish zinc oxide she has applied to her lips and her nose, Carol looks wonderful—more curly and auburn and freckly than ever. She has a piña colada in one hand and a pencil in the other. A thick green notebook rests open against her knees.

Carol has recently finished reading *I'm Okay, You're Okay*. She knows that she and Ernest have helped each other to feel more okay about losing Vince: her long-time lover, Ernest's only friend. Carol believes that she and Ernest have been healing each other's broken hearts. But she's pretty sure that this hasn't yet occurred to Ernest.

Joan has hidden her hair beneath a short brown wig and the hat that looks like a shaggy straw basket. She is wearing a navy-blue shift, heavy white socks, and clunky sandals. The rims of her sunglasses are multicolored and goggle-like. "June" is clearly not a Californian. She's a birdwatcher, maybe, from somewhere else, definitely.

There are binoculars, maps, and a stack of guidebooks at Joan's side, as well as a small styrofoam ice-chest that contains a half-dozen airline-size bottles of vodka. She is lying in the shade of a beach umbrella that bears the name of the hotel where she changed into her costume. She is thinking that she could get used to this—the undercover life.

Ernest is looking forward to later, when he and Carol check into a hotel for an hour or two. Then the long drive home, alone, the good mood, the drink he'll have with his wife on the patio, the desert sunset. Maybe he'll make it with *her*, too. Maybe he'll be up for that.

Carol has her mind on turning points and closures. She trusts what her intuition tells her about the non-physical really close friendship she and Ernest are on the verge of developing.

Two and two was easy for Joan to put together. And the tracking, once she'd decided to see for herself, was a cinch—she could count on her husband to remain a creature of habit. Even so, the baggy red swim trunks are a disappointment.

Joan had imagined—when Ernest had said he had some people to see in Santa Monica, when he didn't explain the beach towel he'd tossed into the car—that he would be wearing something quite different, something tight, and black, and French.

Ernest doesn't like to go to the beach. But when he does go, he always situates himself in the same spot, not too near the water, no matter how many people happen to be close by, impinging—the way they are today.

To his right, a female tourist is apparently asleep beneath her rented umbrella. To his left, a young man and woman sit facing each other. Their eyes are closed. They are pretending to be blind as they touch each other's faces. They are being in love. Ernest would like to throw Carol's notebook at them.

Carol says, "This is like ominous, don't you think? How completely quiet it is, how peaceful everyone seems. You can barely hear the ocean."

Ernest says, "Indian summer. It brings everyone crawling out of the woodwork. What we need is a fence." He glances at the lady tourist, a little embarrassed for her, but mainly relieved that it is not him—fully-clothed, undesirable, by himself. A joke of a human being.

Joan's position is excellent. She can watch without seeming to, hear most of what they say to each other. She knows that her husband would prefer that the beach were empty. She watches him spread suntan oil over his chest and arms. She detects pride in his posture, a definite cockiness. She is almost, for a moment, happy for him.

This is not the first time that Carol has produced her notebook during a rendezvous, writing and reading out loud at the same time: lines of poetry, bits of story, what she calls "found proverbs," like "He who comes too fast has no place else to go." She has assumed all along that Ernest wants to be let in on this activity.

Carol says, "This one's for you, buckaroo. Colon. First paragraph. 'The balmy beach offered herself to him, but the man was not listening. Nor did he perceive the clues left for him amidst the foamy remnants of waves upon the shoreline. Nor did he attend to the sun, who tried to draw him out and soothe him, speaking gently of fall afternoons and fond memories....'"

Ernest is too grateful to Carol to give in to his desire to make fun of her. After all, she calls him "buckaroo." He is filled with gratitude.

As she speaks, he reaches a hand into one cup of her bikini top, then the other. He fondles contemplatively, caught up in the fondling itself—doing such an act, out in the open. Staking his claim in broad daylight. Lovely Carol accommodating him with obliviousness. He hopes that the male partner of the "blind" couple is cheating, is secretly watching this. "Change that to autumnal afternoons," Ernest says to Carol, fingering a nipple. "Autumnal is more poetic."

Joan turns her face away from them and buries it in the blanket in order to stifle her laughter.

Carol says, "You're like completely kidding me, right?" She extracts the hand from her bikini and lays it next to Ernest. "Autumnal my eye!" Carol is smiling, but she takes herself seriously—has been known to say with pride that she has been a writer since the day of her first menstrual period. She closes her journal, steps over her companion, and begins to dig a hole in the sand next to his beach towel.

Ernest closes his eyes and yawns. It is all too clear that what Carol has in mind is to get him into a hole and then cover him with sand. An intolerable game, but he will let her do it. He will let her do just about anything because everything she has done so far has made him feel better. That is, made him feel good. Or at least different. Or if not that much different, at least attended to in ways he had not thought he wanted attending to, and didn't actually need, probably, when you came right down to it. Nevertheless.

Joan watches Carol dig. She admires her friend's doggedness, the no-shilly-shallying practicality with which she pursues her enthusiasms. Joan knows that Carol's hole will not be shallow and half-assed, that Carol will work on it as if she had all the time in the world and yet get it done in a jiffy. Joan wonders what Carol and Ernest have said to each other about the death of Vince.

Ernest wants to keep his mind on the matter at hand. Which is to say, on Carol. He tells himself that, when you came right down to it, sex with Carol is incomparable. Period.

True, the first time, he was probably awkward—not amateurish, needless to say, but probably a bit awkward. He hadn't done it in the back seat of a car, ever, and he wasn't sure that it could be adequately accomplished. And, naturally, he'd been going for the usual lie-down, one knee on the floor of the car, one on the seat, his body hunched over Carol, poised for action despite the stage-fright that was turning his desire into something lopsided and only halfway there. But then she had pushed at him, made him sit up and get comfortable, free to rise, as it were, and he accomplished it all right, and then some.

She had eased herself onto him, into his mighty lap, covering him, tightly wrapping, riding slowly at first, an easy lope to the rhythm of her weeping, to the rhythm of the words she seemed to be chanting—"This is for him, this is for Vince, he loved you, too, you know."

Ernest remembers the words, the effort not to listen to them, the letting it cross his mind that something of Vince might still be up inside her, clinging, waiting for Ernest to get there. And he remembers being appalled by his need, his reach, by the alarming sensation that he was making it not with this woman but with something else, something more important.

Carol likes to dig with her bare hands, especially at the beach. She appreciates the pliability of the sand, the way it gives, the way it moves, as if it wanted to be handled and shaped. She understands that she is similar to the sand in some respects, but that there are significant differences. For one thing, she has a mind of her own. Carol hopes that Ernest, too, will come to see the natural world as an essential source of self-knowledge.

Ernest opens his eyes and looks at the "blind" couple. They are touching each other's hands now. He turns to Carol, on his right, and says loudly that he has some "loins" of poetry for her. He finishes his drink, stretches out on his back, and recites:

> The time has come, the Walrus said,
>   to talk of many things:
> Of sluts and slips and see-through slacks,
>   Of coitus à la king;
> Of why the semen's boiling hot,
>   and whether pigs have flings.

Ernest glances at the "blind" couple. They're looking at him. Both of them. It's about time, he thinks. And now they're gathering their things, getting up, going elsewhere, the wimps. Ernest laughs.

Joan has heard these "loins" of poetry before. She notes that Carol goes on with her work, doesn't give Ernest's performance the time of day. She notes as well that her husband doesn't do the verse that begins with "Marie was wet as wet could be/My wife was dry as dry."

Joan wants to suppose that Ernest is showing some discretion, that he is avoiding any reference to "my wife" and her lubricatory capacities. She also wants to suppose that he has not forgotten that on the occasion of his sharing these bawdy verses with said wife, Joan was wet as wet could be and only the martinis were dry as dry. But the occasion, even so, was not memorable.

Carol dusts off her hands and finally responds to Ernest's poem. She suggests that he take a good long look at what's underneath all that grimy build-up in his head. She is far from being a prude, as he knows, but she can tell a smokescreen when she sees one. Carol is stroking Ernest's arm as she says these things. She means well. She expresses tenderness and concern. Then she steps back over him, grabs the edges of his beach towel, and rolls him into the hole. She says, "My hole is unbelievably perfect!"

Ernest holds his tongue. He doesn't tell her that it's precisely her unbelievably perfect hole that must take some of the blame for his dirty mind. He assuages himself with the explanation that Carol is decidedly youthful—the sort of young woman who speaks of the "flow" one is supposed to "go with" as if she could see it, as if anyone in his right mind could see it.

Ernest tries to picture that flow as Carol would picture it—a gracious river, an oceanic current, maybe a waterfall. But he keeps coming back to his own jizzum, he keeps imagining a ceiling-splashing geyser, nothing middle-aged about it, and so to hell with being in his right mind.

Joan sits up and gets one of the miniature bottles of vodka out of the ice chest. She is not going to be envious of Carol's perfect hole.

She is not going to feel like a kid who has nobody to play with. No pouting, she tells herself. You're in this, and there is nowhere else to go.

She drinks from the bottle and wipes her mouth with the back of her hand. The gesture pleases her: it is just right, "June"-like, desolate but good-natured. One could count on "June" to display an appropriate fastidiousness at the dinner table, but she'd do her outdoor drinking like a trouper. If asked—by fellow travelers on that cruise ship, for instance—she would gladly launch into her disconsolate but inspired version of "I'm in the Mood for Love." Joan imagines Vince on that boat, asking "June" for an encore.

There is a poem in Carol's journal about what happened with Ernest on the day of Vince's funeral—when she couldn't go straight back to the house she and Vince had lived in for eight years, when she didn't know where she wanted to go, when she ended up going into the back seat of Ernest's car. She intends to read the poem to Ernest today, as part of the closure.

Joan does not want to think about Vince in his Smokey-the-Bear outfit getting too close to the forest fire, breathing it in, issuing through his shiny bullhorn excited, longwinded warnings to campers who had long since abandoned their campsites, who knew better than to linger within range of the deadly, insinuating smoke. But Vince would have needed to make sure, would have needed to take care of everybody.

Ernest removes his hat and lets his body settle into the snug, coffin-like hole. He feels extraordinarily cooperative, almost docile. He asks himself whether there might be more to Carol than meets the eye—all that blesséd placidity packaged in a juicy female body. He hopes not.

Carol's poem is a celebration of the life of her dead lover. It's a poem about love and friendship and healing. She hasn't read it to Ernest yet because something told her that he wasn't ready. For one thing, he has never uttered Vince's name. For another, he is always putting his hands on her and really needing her to be there for him physically.

Joan guesses that it started then, on the day of the funeral, this thing between her husband and Carol. She had driven Carol to the service, just the two of them—driving is what Joan could do, it had to take the place of other things, like talking. And driving is what she did when she left before the service was over, when she asked Ernest to give Carol a ride home, then walked briskly down the aisle and out of the chapel as if she had an important appointment. She drove for hours, into the desert, where nothing burns but the sun.

Ernest watches Carol return from the shore toting a plastic bucket filled with water. He assumes three things. One is that Carol prefers a minimum of talk and a maximum of action. Another is that Joan has probably put two and two together and knows better than to rock the boat. The third is that his wife isn't getting any on the side.

Carol packs dampened sand into the spaces beneath Ernest's ankles and knees, under his shoulder blades and neck, around his arms. She is as methodical as a bricklayer. She says, "Once I'm through here, buckaroo, you and me are going to talk."

Joan grins. She is pleased with Carol's foresight, her common-sense approach to having a talk with Ernest. First things first: put him in a hole.

Ernest asks Carol if he is entitled to any last requests. He smiles as he says this in order to make it perfectly clear that he isn't afraid of a little serious verbal intercourse. He sucks in his belly. He is confident that she won't get him to say anything he doesn't want to hear.

Carol says, "Having a talk isn't like getting killed, you know." She shakes her head when Ernest bursts out laughing. "You're unbelievable," she tells him. She smoothes wet sand over his arms and legs and chest, using her hands as trowels, packing him in good and tight.

Joan looks through her binoculars at the horizon. There is nothing to see but the edge. She pretends nevertheless to have sighted something. She opens one of the guidebooks, plays the birdwatcher.

And she remembers an afternoon like this one, late October. She and Vince were sitting in her backyard, waiting for Ernest to get home from work and for Carol who would show up in time for dinner. Vince was talking about the clothes he would design for women if he were a fashion designer: they would all *billow*, he had said, every item, pants, blouses, skirts, dresses, they would float, in every shape and size, every fabric, wools, cottons, silks, synthetics, all year round they would flirt with the breezes, make love with the wind, they would dance like exotic birds. And from the same birds he would develop his color scheme, make the tropical the typical, make all his customers feel like the resplendent quetzal. Imagine it, Vince had said.

Ernest turns his head toward the woman who had been sleeping, he presumed, the one with the ridiculous hat on. He sees her peer through her binoculars and then consult a book. He recognizes this activity, though he himself has never indulged it. He doesn't want to have seen this. The only birdwatcher he has ever known is Vince.

Carol covers Ernest with sand, lots of it. She knows in her heart that Vince would completely understand why she has been spending time with Ernest. Six times, to be exact. This is the seventh. And Vince would be the last person to question how the physical aspect is a natural part of the healing process. Carol believes that Ernest will come through this process a happier person and that Joan will be a major beneficiary of that happiness. So, in a sense, she has included Joan in the process all along—she has, in a sense, been making love to Joan, too, and of course to Vince, in some sense, not to mention, in a way, Ernest.

Ernest has been reminded of the time he and Vince were over in Escondido and Vince spotted the green jay—a genuine event, Vince had said, an unrepeatable sighting, a definite sign, the thing had to be a thousand miles off course, "we're talking a major omen that nobody in his right mind would take lightly," the way Ernest was. And then Vince was saying that the interpretation of the green-jay sign was coming to him, was getting closer, was *here*. "It means the four of us are going to Guatemala, a place I've been aiming to go for some reason unbeknownst. But just between you and me," Vince had said, "that's one of my multitude of nicknames for Carol. Guatemala."

At the time, Ernest took up the topic of the multitude of nicknames and their multitudinous implications, and he'd do the same tomorrow. He knows this. He knows that what he wouldn't have said is that he, Vince, is the genuine event. Unrepeatable. He asks Carol to pour him another drink.

Joan lies down again, rests on her elbows as she sips at a second bottle of vodka and glances over at her husband. The hole is deep. All she can see now is his head, his profile, as Carol holds a glass to his lips. He drinks as if he were thirsty. Something has come over him, Joan is sure of it.

Ernest does not think of Carol as Vince's girlfriend. As Vince's anything. She's a separate item, period. Why muddy the waters? She's just Carol, an available and undemanding woman, not in the least interested in making him account for himself—which he isn't good at in any case, not even when push comes to shove. Maybe she knows this. Vince knows, of course, but he would never let on, or wouldn't let it matter. Joan knows, better than anybody, and lets it matter, but not too much. Joan knows that what he's good at is letting push come to shove. But she can take it. If the need for an accounting should arise, Vince is the one who would come to the rescue, provide the conciliations, help get Ernest off the hook.

It occurs to Ernest that he is not thinking of Vince as dead.

Carol is still piling on the sand, packing it in. She leans over and whispers in Ernest's ear. "Before we leave, maybe we should invite that woman over there to have a drink with us. I mean, did you see her? She's like completely alone."

Joan sees the whispering, and gathers that "June" is being remarked upon, that Carol is probably telling Ernest that "June" is more okay than she looks. Joan imagines Ernest's response: Forget her, tootsie roll. Make like there's no one else on earth but us, babe. Drill a hole down the middle of this grave and give me a lick. It's the Ernest in something tight, and black, and French that Joan is thinking of.

Ernest looks at the bird-watching woman, who is lying down again, but awake, sipping from a small bottle of booze, reading a book. Probably *Peterson's Guide*, like the one Vince kept in his glove compartment. And Ernest thinks: Okay, Vince, maybe I took some kind of advantage. Look at me, buddy, I'm apologizing. It's just that—

Ernest is about to go on in the same vein when he takes another glance at the woman and it dawns on him that he knows that particular sipping. He recognizes the manner, the hand, the mouth. "We're not inviting her," he says to Carol. "No way."

Carol pushes sand onto the mound that covers Ernest and begins to sing a song she has sung once before in his presence, on his behalf, in a hotel room in Palm Springs where they have met three times. On the first of these occasions—their first rendezvous since the car incident—Ernest seemed to Carol to be really anxious. He made jokes about his age, his weight, the possibility that what happened in the car was a fluke, ha ha ha. They were the kinds of jokes that he could laugh at but no one else could.

Joan wonders how Ernest can put up with this singing. His silence on the matter is entirely out of character. Either Carol is awfully good in the sack, or Ernest has lost his mind. In either case, Joan decides, he deserves it, this singing.

Ernest feels trapped. He wants to tell Carol to knock it off. And he wants to tell Joan that she looks ridiculous. He does not want to take his wife's ridiculous presence lying down. He isn't worried that Joan will make a scene. She won't. He knows that. But he's worried that if he doesn't get Carol to stop this goddamned singing, Joan will laugh, and he will hear it.

Carol is letting herself go, putting some guts into it, singing with real oomph about whistling a happy tune whenever you feel afraid.

Ernest is desperate. He asks Carol to give him a kiss, says it as if her song has moved him, deeply. Carol is obliging. Ernest can't move his body, can't put his arms around her, but he is relieved, back in some sort of control of the situation. When she starts to pull away from him, he asks her for another one, and phrases his appeal with care: he asks her this time not for a line of poetry—oh, it was poignant all right, a lyrical kiss—but for a detailed, novelistic smooch.

Carol is kissing Ernest and picturing Vince on the day he taught her the song about not being afraid, back when she feared the under-tow. They had driven from Palm Springs to Laguna and had found a deserted rocky cove for a picnic, just enough dry sand to accommodate their blanket. Gradually, bit by are-we-really-doing-this bit, they found themselves undressing each other, ignoring the sandwiches and the beer, heeding nothing but being in love while the tide came in and in. And then a roaring, rock-tumbling wave swept under and over them, carrying their lunch out to sea, and Vince had said, "Let's go in, she's requesting our company, I'll bring you back safe, I promise" and he sang the song as they went into the water and let the currents carry them out.

Ernest is kissing a preoccupied Carol and looking at his wife, hoping that she will get the point and pack up her props and go home. He can deal with her later. He is plenty angry with her for making bird-watching part of her act, shoving Vince in his face like that. And he'll let her know it, later, no holds barred. At the moment, though, he wants more than anything to get out from under this mound of sand that is keeping his arousal from fully expressing itself.

Joan is watching them kiss. She can't tell whether Ernest's shaded eyes are open or shut, but they don't appear to be engaged in the kissing. The mirrored sunglasses are in fact turned in her direction. Perhaps he is aware that she is watching. Perhaps he wants her to watch. Yes. That's it.

Joan knows that she has been found out. She waves to her husband.

Carol draws back and sits cross-legged on Ernest's beach towel. She shapes her own towel into a pillow and places it under his head. She knows that this isn't easy for him—letting her have her way with him, imagining how silly he must look with only his head poking out of the sand. So she runs her finger through Ernest's graying hair, gives his bearded cheeks a tender pat, and opens her journal. She says, "Okay. Here we go, humdinger. Second paragraph. Colon. 'The sand, the sea, the sun, the sky, and the auburn-haired woman worked together as one, in natural harmony, to lift the man's spirit and reveal himself to himself, but he was not ready.'"

Ernest says, "Ready or not, here I come." But his heart isn't in it. He wishes he had saved that line for later. The trouble is, he can't see Joan. He doesn't know what she is up to. Carol is blocking his view.

What's going on?

Joan is removing the navy-blue shift. She has taken off the hat, the wig, the sunglasses, the sandals and socks. Under the shift is a brand new peacock-colored two-piece swimsuit with a breezy ruffle at the bodice and the hips. She gets three bottles of vodka out of the ice chest, one for each of them.

Carol writes and speaks. "'Nevertheless, the man began to have a mysterious feeling, as if something were about to happen, a turning point, as when the weather suddenly changes, and he senses a gathering of clouds, a mournful wind, a startling downpour.'"

That wave of the hand, those teasing fingers—Ernest has to know what Joan is doing. He tells himself that she has to be doing just what he wants her to be doing—going away, leaving him alone, not letting this thing matter too much. After all, she's his Joanie. But he is imagining a concealed weapon.

Ernest looks at Carol, at her lovely breasts and stomach. He tries to pay attention to what is supposed to be on the agenda. He tries to keep the priorities straight, to forget about his wife. Ernest says, "What happens after the downpour?"

Joan says, "We shoot you" as she sits on the mound of sand beneath which her husband is buried. "After we give you the option of taking it in the head or the heart." Joan puts on her husband's new cowboy hat.

Carol smiles, sits next to Joan, and gives her a hug.

Ernest says, "But I survive. You flub the job. The gun doesn't go off. I plot revenge on the both of you."

Joan opens the tiny bottles and says, "Actually, darling, what happens after the downpour is that you are cleansed—isn't that about right, Carol?—and we all live happily ever after."

Joan dusts some sand from Ernest's brow and briefly caresses his cheek. "Carol had no idea that I would show up. She is entirely innocent," Joan tells her husband. "Drinks are on me."

Carol starts to cry. She is crying and telling Joan about how she and Ernest were about to begin a non-physical close friendship, the next stage in the healing process. Carol offers to read the poem she has written about all of it.

Ernest says, "No poems. Please. And I do not need to be healed, I need to be released from this hole." He sounds calm, but he isn't. He pictures himself buried like this for hours, days, two beautiful women in their two-piece bathing suits sitting atop the mound that covers him, touching each other the way women do, consoling, talking things over as if he weren't there, all that female flesh exposed and self-contained, unreachable, and somehow extracting from him promises that he would not otherwise make. He is outnumbered, outfoxed. And with a heavy, painful tremor for which he is utterly unprepared, he longs for his dead friend.

Vince is dead, he tells himself.

Ernest tries to fight it off. There are tears in his eyes, but he says, "Plan B. You two take turns sitting on my face."

Carol is crying. "Maybe it's like completely hopeless," she says to Joan.

Joan looks at her husband. She sees what there is to see there, which is not the impudence he intends but a grief-stricken appeal that tells her all about the thing between him and Carol. And Vince.

Joan gets up, leaves them for a moment, then returns to her spot on the mound with the unbecoming hat and the wig and the touristy sunglasses. "May I?" she says to Ernest. "You'll feel better."

Ernest says, "Yes. Put them on me."

Carol says, "I don't understand."

Joan says, to Ernest, "I called her 'June.'"

Ernest says, "I'll call her 'Dick.'" He laughs, sort of.

But Joan was right—the silly disguise makes him feel better. Like somebody new, from somewhere else, who is having a wonderful time.

* * *

In their spacious Spanish-style house, with its wide archways, its dark beams, and its surrounding wall of dense oleander, Joan and Ernest get ready for work, or they come home from work, or they do bookwork in preparation for the next day's work—she as the "imaginatively conservative" owner of an elegant and expensive dress shop; he as a member of a "high-powered" consulting team whose principal client is one of the major oil companies. That is how they are described by the Palm Springs Chamber of Commerce, whose invitations they always ignore.

She is increasingly afraid that something is happening to her: she will be standing at the kitchen counter, washing the asparagus or the artichokes, her hands occasionally resting on the lovely dark-blue tiles, and she will be trying to make a mental list of the next day's have-tos, but the list won't stick. It's as if her mind were made of something slippery and delicate. She will be trimming the asparagus or stuffing the artichokes, and she will try again, this shouldn't be so difficult, thinking about tomorrow, about the things that need doing. But she can't make it happen. Maybe, she tells herself, she ought to go to bed early—yes, she'll do that, she'll go to bed early.

After work he sometimes looks at the plate glass windows that provide an expansive view of the big backyard, the patio, and the pool, and he sometimes wants to see those windows shattered into a thousand pieces, wants to hear the crash, and then another, wants to break each one of them with his own body, wants to hurl himself, and then do a triumphant dance upon the splintered remains. Some day, he thinks, he'll do that, yes, he'll boogey-woogey all over the wreckage.

Meanwhile, they move through the house like spirits, touching without being touched, their bare feet or their stockinged feet whispering along the ceramic floors—whispering tales, perhaps, about the times when it is not so quiet.

* * *

It Had to Be You

As they entered the county courthouse Joan said to her husband that if it were not for this brutal murder they might have forgotten their anniversary altogether.

To which Ernest replied, "Indeedy."

But Joan did not feel witty. She remembered, vaguely, the faces she had seen on the local news the night before. Faces that belonged to a section of the county she had never visited. Where they lived in trailer parks. The diminutive parents of the murdered child. The bearded, delicate defendant.

Ernest had called them animals. Then he had laughed and said, "Which reminds me. Our anniversary was last week." He had watched his wife's face as he added, "We'll go out tomorrow. For lunch. Take the day off."

Joan had stared at the television. The cameraman was showing her the back of someone's head, reddish shoulder-length hair fixed in a limp pageboy. The defendant's wife.

It was Joan who had said, "After lunch, let's go to the trial."

"An all-out celebration." Ernest liked the idea.

Joan knew that she would have to hear things, see things. The rope with which the victim had been tied to the fence.

Perhaps Joan wasn't smiling as they entered the county courthouse because Ernest *was*.

What she told herself was, I can take it.

They had lunched on smoked trout at the country club. Joan felt strong in her camel-colored cashmere and her heavy gold bracelets. One for each wrist.

So she was the one who got things going. She teased her husband, egged him on, stopped just short of saying "go for it." "It" being their attractive middle-aged waitress, a waitress their own age. Though better preserved, Joan remarked, longer *cured*. A waitress Ernest described, to amuse his wife, as a T-bone. A working man's piece. A waitress who could not disguise her interest in Joan's husband.

"It's your patch," Joan said. She wore a crooked smile on her narrow face. "She likes your patch."

Ernest had once, in college, for the first few months of his senior year, worn a patch over his left eye. In order to attract the sensitive women. The wound as magnet. As honey. It worked, of course. He told this to Joan after it had really happened. After his eye, the other one, had been caught and ruined with a fishhook.

Ernest did not treasure the moment when his lure had suddenly given in to his pull. When it had loosened itself from the entangling edge of the lake and had snapped back too quickly. Whipped into him without warning. But he relished the look on Joan's face when he told her the story of his college prank. He had laughed at the moral of the story.

Joan had not laughed. She considered herself a sensitive woman. Like those college women who had found his wound appealing. The imagined pain of it compelling.

Which is why Joan suspected all along that she was the responsible party. That it had been the lure she had given him. A spontaneous present, a gesture of camaraderie—extravagantly feathered and fierce, in its own special case. The kind of thing a fisherman's wife would buy. A fancy hook. "For the big one," Joan had told him.

Ernest, when he had returned to the California desert from his fisherman's dream of a trip to the Canadian lakes, his right eye gone, his sunburned face half obscured with bandages that looked to Joan as if they had memory, had only said, "You should have seen the one that got away."

It was two weeks before Joan asked, "Which lure?"

"El Bularo," Ernest said. He made martinis.

Joan knew the name. She had read in the newspapers about the infamous bull, run through to the heart, buckling at the knees, going down, dead, but in his death taking one last swipe at the bowing matador. Killing the winner. El Bularo. The Joker.

"El Bularo does not answer my question."

"Never mind," Ernest said to his wife. "Suspense is good."

About the waitress Ernest remarked, "She isn't very subtle, is she?"

Joan looked at her husband, at his wavy graying hair. Since the accident he had let it grow wild. Joan imagined the waitress putting her petite, pretty hands into that hair. Then putting her face in it. In Ernest's Byronic hair.

Joan had thoughts.

"Can't dissemble worth a damn," Ernest repeated.

"She's enchanted," Joan said. She almost smiled as if to suggest, I know whereof I speak.

"By the wicked sorcerer." Ernest lifted the dark eyebrow over his good eye. He liked this game.

And so did Joan, in a sense. Insofar as she could call the shots.

"Little does she know," Joan said, "how wicked." She held her husband's gaze. Two eyes to one. She felt like a dangerous woman. A character in a foreign film, all these years.

Ernest raised his glass. He made a toast to his wife who kept him *en garde*, kept him fit. "Happy sixteenth or whatever it is," he said.

Joan touched her glass to her husband's. Champagne. A festive occasion. "Has it been that long? I've completely forgotten."

That would do for retort, even though it was true. Joan no longer counted days or months or years. She did not count much of anything.

"*Touché*," said her husband.

Ernest felt good. Leslie, the waitress—who had let it slip that she was fifty-one, that she could bench-press seventy-five pounds, ten reps, no sweat, and that she could filet all manner of fish with her eyes closed—made Ernest feel good.

And so, in a different way, of course, did Joan.

Ernest had words for Joan. Joan was "classic." Joan was "expensive." Joan was "subtle." Joan was "thirsty." Joan was a "ball-breaker." Joan was "titless."

When Leslie returned to their table she looked at Ernest. As if she knew him, Joan thought. As if they knew each other.

"How is everything?" Leslie asked.

"The trout was lovely," Joan said.

Ernest chuckled. "She means delicious."

Leslie laughed along with Ernest. "I know what she means," Leslie said.

Joan arranged her knife and fork on her empty plate.

Ernest went on. "It's a *live* thing," he said to Leslie, "a thing that's got *life* to it—that's what I call lovely." He looked at the waitress with an eye that set the hook. An eye that told a story. A love story that did not end happily but was worth it.

Joan half wanted to interrupt what was going on. Everybody's focus on Leslie's "thing." She also half wanted to watch, to assist. She wondered what Leslie would say if she were to see what was hidden beneath Ernest's patch. Joan half wanted to dare Ernest to do it. To show Leslie what wasn't there.

But instead she said, "The dead fish was delicious."

"That's more like it!" Ernest finished his champagne.

Joan believed that if she were ever to slap her husband she would do it on the left side of his face. So that he could see it coming. "Wonderful you," she told him.

Leslie winked at Joan's husband and said, "I'll get you two love-birds some coffee."

Inside the courthouse Joan and Ernest sat a few rows back from the prosecutor's table. On the same side where the jury sat. Where the parents and friends of the murdered child sat. Two dozen people at most. Joan wondered if they wondered why she and Ernest were there.

Across the aisle Joan saw the hair of the defendant's wife. The wife's limp hair rested on beefy shoulders. The defendant's wife was large. Much larger than the defendant. There was a large man sitting next to her. A brother, perhaps. An ally. Joan could not see the wife's face.

But she saw the face of the defendant when he was escorted into the courtroom by two elderly marshals. And Joan had two thoughts. One was that the red-faced, paunchy marshals looked comically alike. A vaudeville team. The other was that the defendant looked like Jesus Christ.

Ernest had one thought.

He whispered to Joan, "They should do to him what he did to her."

"Yes," Joan responded. "An eye for an eye."

Ernest grinned. He squeezed his wife's hand.

Joan whispered, "I've never been in the same room with a murderer before."

Ernest said nothing.

So Joan added, "That I know of."

It was the third day of the trial. Joan heard a man behind her say that the prosecutor would be winding things up.

Things, Joan said to herself. That you wind up. Nothing to it.

They heard the testimony of a reluctant but apparently voluntary witness. A man Ernest described as a "derelict." The derelict was unshaven. He was on edge. He appeared to be wearing somebody else's suit. He swore that he had seen the suspect's car, with the girl in it, on the morning of the crimes in question.

Joan did not think about the crimes in question. She thought about "derelict." Abandoned. Forsaken. Bereft.

The defense attorney asked the derelict if it was true that he had once been jailed for attempted assault with a deadly weapon. For an attempted assault on his wife, with his skinning knife. To which the derelict replied, "It was true, sir."

"That took guts," Ernest whispered.

Joan assumed that her husband was referring to the derelict's voluntary testimony.

But Ernest added, "I wonder if he meant to scalp her." He watched his wife's face as he said this. But she did not flinch.

Joan, as far as she knew, never flinched.

They heard the testimony of a medical examiner. A thin woman with dark brown hair. A woman Ernest described as "sexless." Who explained the procedures by which semen samples are evaluated and compared. Who identified the semen samples taken from the girl's jeans and T-shirt and sweater and underpants. Who said that the girl had not been penetrated. Who said "That is correct" each time the prosecutor held a piece of evidence before her and asked if she had examined it. Who said nothing as the prosecutor handed each piece of evidence to the jury. The girl's jeans, her T-shirt, her sweater, her jacket, her pink tennis shoes, her socks, her underpants sealed in a small plastic bag. The rope with which the girl had been tied to a fence in a remote corner of one of the golf courses.

Ernest nudged his wife. "Look."

"I'm looking." Joan was looking at each numbered item that was being passed from one member of the jury to the next. From one pair of ordinary hands to the next. She was looking at their faces as they touched the evidence. The clothes the girl had worn. On her way to school. On the day she had been kidnapped, not penetrated, re-clothed, strangled, tied to a fence.

Re-clothed. Joan was looking at the clothes the man had put back on the girl. The medical examiner had said so. Everything off, then on. Mis-buttoned and inside-out. That's how they knew. He had put her pink tennis shoes back on. Onto the wrong feet.

Somebody had done that.

Joan saw the whole thing. Saw herself as the victim. Not penetrated. Impervious. She saw herself as the man who looked like Jesus Christ. Saw herself putting on the clothes, doing it all the wrong way, not knowing what she was doing. She saw the defendant's wife standing beside her. Saw that she was not forsaken. The wife would help her take care of things. Wind things up.

Ernest nudged her again. "Look."

The large man was gone. He could not take it, Joan decided. One could see the wife now, if one looked. Which Joan did not do.

She looked instead at the defendant. His face was blank as he watched the members of the jury touch the girl's clothes. As he watched them handle the rope. Joan thought, He still looks like Jesus Christ but he also looks like no one.

Joan did not think of herself as a religious person.

She did not look at the defendant's wife.

They made arrangements for another day away from work.

As they entered the county courthouse for the second time, Joan said to her husband, "I don't want to see her."

"I dreamt we had her over," Ernest said. "For dinner."

Joan knew what he wanted her to think. He wanted her to think "had her for dinner." She knew Ernest's dreams. She knew that he believed it was a good thing to have bad dreams, sick dreams. She knew that he believed she had problems because she tried not to dream at all.

"I'm surprised," Joan told him.

"At what?"

"That you dreamt about beefsteak. Not T-bone."

"And not cold cuts."

Joan said nothing.

"Meaning you-know-who."

Joan knew.

They moved toward the row they sat in the day before.

Joan did not take off her sunglasses.

Ernest patted his wife's ass. As if she were on his team.

Joan kept her eyes on the witnesses for the defense. The well-groomed experts who explained inconclusively why the prosecutor's material evidence was inconclusive. Then four character witnesses who said that the defendant was a man of good character. A man who loved his wife. A man who took uncommon interest in his wife's career as a dental assistant. A man who went to church, who got on well with children, who was incapable of violence.

Witnesses to nothing, Joan thought. To character.

The defendant was put on the stand. His voice was meek. He sounded depressed. Not sad. Joan knew the difference between depressed and sad. She wondered if the jury knew the difference. If they would be fooled. If they would look at the defendant's face and listen to his voice and think about who shall inherit the earth.

"Look," Ernest whispered.

Joan thought, If he were totally blind this wouldn't happen. He wouldn't try to be boss. He would be incapable.

"Get it over with," said Ernest.

Joan refused. She listened to the defendant. The defendant was saying "Yes, sir" to everything his attorney asked him. Yes, sir, he never picked that girl up in his car. Yes, sir, he never did any of those things. Yes, sir, he had been married about a year. Yes, sir, he could not recall exactly how long. Yes, sir, he never killed that girl.

Yes, Joan said to herself. Sir.

Then the defendant was saying "Yes, sir" to the prosecutor. Yes, sir, he was hanging out with friends that morning. Yes, sir, he had a couple of friends. Yes, sir, he could not recall their last names. Yes, sir, he would call himself a shy person. Yes, sir, he was not so shy around children.

"What an asshole," whispered Ernest.

Joan thought he might be referring to the defendant, or to the defense attorney who had put his client on the stand. Or to everyone, in general.

But she asked, "Me?"

"Who else?"

Joan did not take this bait. She did not look at the defendant's wife. She already knew what she would see. A wife who would take care of things. Who would never let things become public. Who would bury the evidence. Who would never be found out. Who could take it. Who could take "I'll get you two lovebirds some coffee." Who would never let on that she knew that she was beefy. Who would straighten her husband's tie just before the execution.

The defendant's wife, Joan thought, was a dangerous woman.

"Our guy's a devil," Ernest told her. It was a compliment aimed at the prosecutor. The prosecutor was good. He was wily. He was handsome. He was intimate.

Joan saw that the prosecutor was making the defendant fall in love with him. That he was making the defendant want to tell him everything. Out of love.

But all the defendant said was, "It never happened."

"He didn't tell," Joan said to her husband.

"You're all alike." Ernest laughed.

Ernest was happy. He was certain his side would win. "He'll fry," he said.

As they left the courtroom Joan looked at the defendant's wife.

The defendant's wife was smiling.

"She's been at it the whole time," Ernest said.

"I know."

It was not a broad smile. It was not a fake smile. It reminded Joan of the first smile she had ever sliced into a jack-o'-lantern. A toothless smile. A sliver of a grin across a wide blank face. A secret. A cut.

Ernest told her, "It reminds me of brides."

Joan did not respond to this.

Joan was incapable of violence.

She said, "She's smiling that way because her husband gets on so well with children."

Joan was such a kidder. Ernest liked that. He liked Joan. "El Bularo," he said to his wife. Called her that, affectionately.

* * *

    She said to him one night as they sat with their drinks on the patio that she had always disliked her name. That the only thing more dull, more plain than Jane was Joan. If her parents had named her after Joan of Arc, maybe, she said, it would be a little easier to live with, only a little. But it was Joan Crawford they had in mind.
    He said that he didn't dislike his name. He despised it. It linked him up in people's minds with either Wilde or Hemingway: "A queer or a suicide." People make the connection, he said, he was sure of it.
    He hated his name.
    When you think about it, he told her, you're lucky. Yours is just a name, no frills, nothing to make people get any ideas. Besides, you're clearly not a Mary or a Rachel. And there are plenty of names out there that are worse than Joan. Names that nobody in his right mind would want to try to live with. Think of Heidi. Or Melody. Or Abigail. If you can see yourself as a Ruby or a Gloria, then I don't know you from Adam.
    Joan had done it again—said only a piece of a thought, kept the rest to herself, knowing that the rest, if spoken, would seem silly. She smiled at the ambivalent evening sun, and at the way Ernest managed to toy with her unsaid thoughts. She had been thinking about a beautiful brown woman who works at the grocery store: a checker whose greetings were so open and pacific, whose simple white headscarf signified duty and devotion, a whole way of life. This woman's name was Jasmine.

* * *

Where or When

Joan wants to finish decorating the Christmas tree.

Ernest wants to get laid.

Ordinarily, Joan would host a small holiday party for her employees at the store, amidst whatever remained of the lush red cashmeres and the sequined dresses. Female staff only, four full-time, two-part time. Champagne and caviar after closing on Christmas Eve. Genial farewells to the aftertaste of the sales pitch. Stylish shoes kicked off. Bonuses discreetly tucked into gold-ribboned boxes of French perfume.

Ordinarily, Ernest would consider other "outlets," as he called them. And he might, now and then, act upon those considerations. But he doesn't feel like doing that. Something is going on here, in his own home, which requires his attention, an assertion of some sort.

Joan had agreed with Ernest, from the start, to resist the pull of other people's nostalgias and traditions, which had nothing to do with their lives. They had never, ergo, put up a tree in the house at Christmas.

Now Joan is rocking the boat. She is having the employees' party at the house. A Sunday buffet dinner. Holly and red roses for a centerpiece. Juniper and white lilies at the bar. A ten-foot Carolina fir. Poinsettias around the pool, the front door, and the fireplace.

The invitations included the seamstress, the delivery man, the stock boy whose wardrobe apparently consisted of nothing but a white t-shirt and gaudily-flowered swim trunks. Everyone's spouse or companion was welcome. The salesgirls could talk of nothing else. They couldn't wait to see the boss lady's house.

Joan assumes that she must have been out of her mind when she decided to do this, to trust the impulse. The sentiment, of all things. But it's too late. Everyone is coming. She wonders what the stock boy will wear.

Ernest says, "How long is this going to take?"

"I don't know," Joan tells him. "I haven't done this since I was a kid. And even then, I mainly watched."

They had argued about the party. Joan announced after the fact that she had mailed out invitations, ordered a tree. Ernest said that she had no right to change their routine on her goddamn own. He wanted an explanation. He would agree to the party but not to the tree, the lights, the goddamn decor. Joan assured him that the party signaled no significant change in the routine. He said bullshit. She said have it your way. He said he just might not show up. She said it'll be all right, you'll see. Et cetera. He had looked, in his good eye, which was whitened and stretched, as if he were going to weep, or scream. Joan patted him on the shoulder and told him not to worry.

Ernest is worried because something seems to have come over his wife. It's as if she were wrapped in a blanket that he has never seen before, that she has been keeping in storage all this time, privately. He wants to get it off her and get laid.

Joan is standing on a small stepladder, winding a string of white lights into the uppermost branches. Trying not to let the wiring show. Trying not to feel the nearness of her husband, who is standing with his hands in his pockets right behind her. Behind her behind.

She is aware that she has missed the smell of such a tree in the house. She is also aware that menopause has come upon her like a show-off autumn in Vermont that makes remembering irresistible.

She remembers her father as he stood in adoring attendance, a box of gleaming golden bells in his hands. Her mother barefoot on a tapestried stool, gaily fussing over the placement of each ornament, reaching, so that her red sweater would hike up and reveal her creamy, girlish midriff.

Joan imagines herself falling gently forward off the ladder, falling into the smell, lying on and within the slender branches, the welcome touch of the soft butch-haircut pine needles. The embrace would snap a few of the brittle twigs, releasing tart evergreen juice.

She sees the pretty faces of her saddle-shoed elementary school classmates—were they as fearless as they had seemed then?—who told in whispers of sneaking late at night into living rooms or dens, turning on the Christmas tree lights, making a heavenly temple there in the dark, aglow with promise. They told of scooching in under the lowest branches, as careful as new nuns, then looking up, wishing they could live there always, planning grown-up lives for themselves that would be like that, all colors and lights.

It is mid-afternoon, sunny but chilly enough to warrant a fire in the fireplace once the guests begin to arrive. Joan has bathed but not yet fixed her hair or applied her make-up. She is wearing a short terrycloth robe. Thick and white. There is Ella Fitzgerald, not too loud, in the background, singing love songs. Joan feels both reckless and as patient as a cloud, not displeased that they call this The Change.

Ernest wants to put his hands on her. A thumb on each buttock, palms spread over the hip bones, fingers pressing the thin, softening pelvis that is hidden beneath the robe. His own blond bundle of white, his lamb, his goddamn wife. He could easily lift her off the ladder, carry her into the bedroom. We could play—he smiles at the thought—Santa Claws.

"You look good," Ernest says.

"Would you please turn the heat down on the cous-cous?"

"Turn the heat down."

"Yes. Thanks."

Ordinarily, Ernest would not comply with such a request in a manner that might be taken for domestic cooperation. That might give the impression, in this case, that he had changed his mind about the party. About gratuitous goodwill and strangers in his house and Christmas as such. He has not changed his mind. But he is worried. So this time he does what Joan asks, without further comment. He wishes that he could tell himself that he was heading for the kitchen, per instructions, because he was pussy-whipped.

Knight-errant Ernest moves the dial on the stove from medium to low. He imagines such a dial implanted in some convenient spot on his wife's aloof, alluring, middle-aged body. Convenient to him, that is, not to her. Like that place in the middle of her back where zipping up or zipping down is almost impossible for her to achieve by herself. She has to ask him to do it. He is needed there. That's clearly the spot, he thinks, for the silver dial. Low, medium, high. On and off. What a life.

Ernest gives himself a heaping spoonful of the cous-cous. Tumeric, mint, and lemon. Tender lamb and onions. Fresh tomatoes and garlic. He can taste none of it, the stuff is far too hot. His eyes fill with tears. He opens his mouth and sucks in air in order to cool it off. Then he takes another spoonful.

Joan plugs in the lights and stands back for a look.

Ernest stands at the stove and eats, planning his next move.

When she decided to give this party, Joan was gnawing on a secret, thinking about Molly, about not losing her. Molly: manager of the store for fifteen years, from the beginning. Tall, willowy, self-contained Molly. Sixty-four and effortlessly sexy. In sync with her boss in taste, in temperament, in bottom lines. It's not that they are friends—they're not, in the usual sense. It's better than that, Joan would say.

If Molly has a personal life, nobody knows much about it, or wants to. The salesgirls, otherwise good-natured gossips, like her just the way she is: as quietly elegant and standoffish as Joan, but surrounded by an unmistakable aura of musk. Never talkative, but always dream-provoking. "Once upon a tempestuous time," she told them, "I was a runway model. Paris. Milan. New York. End of story." Or this: "Once upon a torch song time, I was married to a matador. Imagine the unwrapping of him, if you will." And they did.

The thing is, Molly recently told Joan that she would like to retire come the new year. Go sailing in the South Pacific. Spend her savings on the acquisition of new metaphors. Fall in love one last time. "These right-hand-man times have been tip top," she explained. "But my times are running out. I'd best get on with it."

Ordinarily, Joan would not panic. But she had been to-the-bone startled by Molly's announcement. Startled, that is, by her own reaction. By how close she came to pleading. By the ache, which she should long since have predicted and prepared for. She brooded for days over what went wrong, why she had failed to see another ending coming round the bend.

What went wrong was that nothing did. The virtual partnership with Molly Baines had been consistently seemly and inspired. They glided through their work days like a couple of steel-plated swans, all symmetry and success. Not one unsafe, unguarded moment. So that Joan forgot to consider the possibilities. So that she found herself having to persuade Molly not to leave, not yet, and persuade without turning herself into a squawking lesser fowl.

Hence the party. Joan is going a-wooing. She is out of her mind, but it is good, almost. She has arranged everything the way her mother would have: sure-fire recipes, the right wines, an amiable bartender, thoughtful presents for everyone, music, flowers, the whole shebang. Including, for Molly, a gallant late-fiftyish French sportswear manufacturer now working out of L.A. and weekending in Palm Springs.

Joan spent the morning wrapping dollops of curried shrimp in filo dough, cutting two legs of lamb into neat, nearly fatless cubes. Now she stands before the lighted tree and opens a box of brand new ornaments, satiny white globes, and emerald, and edible red that she will nestle among the lights, among the fluffs of angels. She feels dewy and plump, too ripe for her own good.

Ernest returns to the living room with two drinks and three delicate parcels of shrimp. He sets the drinks down on the stepladder and eats the hors d'oeuvres.

"You almost done?"

"No. I'll be a while."

"When are they coming?"

"Six-thirty."

"There's plenty of time."

"Do you want to give me a hand?"

"Yes. Both of them. Nice-nice." Ernest sucks in his stomach.

Joan sees her mother's exposed midriff, the slender waist, and the look in her father's eyes that spoke both a desire to touch and a need to restrain himself, as though his beautiful wife were more wonder than fact, more angel than flesh, liable to vanish if caressed by mortal hands. And Joan remembers that her mother had turned around on the tapestried footstool, had seen the look, had reached out for him and brought his face into her soft sweater-covered breasts, and had held him there, her fingers in his hair, for a long time.

Joan hands Ernest one of the drinks and a box of ornaments. She moves her drink from the stepladder to the coffee table, without taking a sip.

"Why aren't you drinking? We drink in this family."

"I don't know," Joan says. "I'm not thirsty." She remounts the stepladder.

"Since when?"

"I'm just not." She repositions one of the ornaments she'd already hung.

Ernest looks up at her. "So the idea is, I'm supposed to stand here like a gentleman and serve you the decorations."

"In a way, yes. That's the idea."

Joan feels as if she were floating, hovering above a Christmas scene in which there is a woman and a man, more old than young, and perhaps always so, and yet who from the hovering distance appear to be children, a boy and a girl pretending to be the wife in her bathrobe and the husband in his best crew-neck sweater, and the poor things don't know how to do this at all.

As a rule, Ernest is not suspicious when it comes to his wife. If he knows one thing, it's that Joan is not the type to fall in love. She's a cut-your-losses-in-advance type. The best type. No whimsies. No leaps. Nothing out-of-the-blue. Until now he was sure that she was not and never would be an angels-in-the-Christmas-tree type. Which makes him suspicious.

Joan is steamy inside her robe, a little dizzy, which she tells herself is the menopause talking, and not memory, though the two seem to have become twin sisters: an inseparable and flushed pair of women who go naked all the time and braid each other's hair and have minds of their own.

She listens to the music and thinks about Molly and the Frenchman. She imagines that they will not let on that they are instantly smitten. They will glide about the house, maintaining a decorous and impassioned distance between them. They will exchange an unobserved and ever-remembered glance when Ella sings *"the smile you are smiling you were smiling then, but I can't remember where or when."* Cut it out, Joan tells herself. You are becoming a perspiring version of your powder-puff mother, who was so embarrassingly susceptible to love songs. Just cut it out.

Joan is nevertheless humming Ella's music.

Ernest drinks and, with a bow, proffers the box of ornaments. "I think we should have some sex," he says. "Before the party."

"What?"

"You heard me."

Joan turns in order to look at him, at that tone of voice. She sees that his patch has hiked up a bit, as it might on a little kid dressed up as a pirate. There is a miserable grin on his face. She takes an ornament from the box. She is too warm for this, can't think straight.

"I've got Molly on my mind, Molly Baines," she says. "Remember Molly? I think you met her once, not here, somewhere. She wants to quit her job, do other things, adventures. I seem to be frantic about it." Joan reaches up into the branches, hangs an ornament, and keeps on talking. "I didn't see it coming. I'm not ready for her to leave. Does that make any sense? I've arranged for a man to be here tonight that I want her to meet. I want them to form an attachment. So that she'll stay. Me the matchmaker, it's hard to fathom but there it is. I'm cultivating lovebirds, or whatever it is you do with them."

"Be all that as it may," Ernest says, "you heard me."

Joan is out of breath. And far too visible. Yes, she heard him. And she remembers looking away but being unable to leave the room as her parents held each other there in front of the Christmas tree. She had looked away, after a while, because she could not keep on looking at the sad part of grown-up loving that a special kind of reaching for each other was supposed to banish but didn't.

Joan takes the box of decorations from Ernest's hand. She doesn't face him this time, doesn't want to show him everything. "I need to get this done," she says. "Then I have to dress. The bartender will be here at six to set things up."

Joan sees herself at twenty-two, draped for a while in the gauzy textures of romance, almost a believer in that special kind of reaching for each other, almost a dreamer of some breezy place where lovers always loved and no one ever died. That was before she met Ernest, before she knew that she could become the Joan who could become his wife. Who could get over it, get tough, get laid, get old.

"I'm sorry," she tells him.

Ernest finishes his drink and sets it down on the coffee table next to Joan's. Then he comes up behind her and puts his arms around her, tries to loosen the belt on her robe, leans his face against her buttocks.

"Don't be sorry," he says. "Be Joan."

Ordinarily, that is, she would just do it.

For one thing, the occasions were rare. For another, there was nothing like it as a cure for memory. She became, while it lasted, and for some time thereafter, no one, a nameless body, an orphan born deaf to the language of lovers. This was comforting, most of the time.

At the moment, she feels as if those unruly twin sisters had strung row after row of tiny white lights inside her body. She is lit-up and overfull, liable to give into something, arouse a pack of sleeping dogs.

"Later," she says.

"No. Now."

Ernest lifts her off the ladder and puts his hands up under her robe, clutching at her waist, pulling her to him. He grabs at her panties. "O come all ye faithful," he half-sings.

Joan's hands struggle with Ernest's, but it is as if hers were nothing more than the sidekick, going along for the ride, grabbing with his grab, touching whatever he touches. The panties, the cheeks of her bottom, belly button, pubic hair. Fighting over the toys, she thinks, as she sees those children again, the boy and the girl, each of them wanting something that has nothing to do with the toys, grappling and afraid of themselves, sullen in victory.

Ernest is breathing sour puffs of shrimp and scotch into Joan's face. She lets go of his hands and tries to heave herself free, but then he has her again from around the back and he has her arms pinned close against her stomach and he is pressing himself into her robe, into the cleavage of her buttocks. "O come let us adore him," he says.

Joan kicks out in front of her, wildly, a whirligig, a cartoon character, and she knows it. Who are these people, she wonders. And yet she keeps on kicking her thin, no longer youthful legs, going along with it, this madness, until she kicks the stepladder over and it crash-lands into a box of crystal stars.

"Okay," she says.

"Okay what?"

Ernest doesn't let go, but he relaxes his hold, tries to pull off a segue into a caress. He's still puffing, and he is surprised that he doesn't feel more exhilarated, more erect.

"Okay, enough of this." Joan turns within his arms to face him, this man, her husband. Mate, she thinks, to her yellow-bellied soul. She puts her fingers on the back of his neck, tries to steady herself, tries not to imagine what it might be like, with Ernest, to do this in that other way. But she imagines it. And it is better than comforting.

Ernest pulls her closer, humming the Christmas carol about the faithful, doing his best to keep up the momentum, to downplay his part as the heavy. What counts is that his wife is looking at him as if she wants it.

Joan kisses her husband. "Make love to me," she whispers. "Let's make love."

Ernest steps back. "What's that supposed to mean?" He gets himself out of the embrace and picks up the drink that Joan didn't drink. "What are you trying to pull?"

Ordinarily, Joan wouldn't pass up such a sweet opportunity to say "your leg, of course." But she is speechless, too far out on the wrong limb. The thing now is to become as light as a wood nymph, inch back, don't let this cradle fall. She has never felt so foolish, not ever. She'll ask her doctor about hot flashes, medication.

Ernest says, "I won't be manipulated, missy."

He finishes his drink and goes to the bar to make them both another. There is an elaborate tray of cheeses there, coming to room temperature. So he eats while he fixes the drinks. All he wants is peace of mind. Is that too much to ask? He could have gotten a good hard-on to prove it, if she hadn't made him feel like some kind of brute. Make love to me—goddamn her. Pulling that stuff. All he wants is for Joan not to go crazy and do something stupid. Like go off on adventures with what-d'ya-call-it Molly.

Joan more or less makes it back, more or less safe and sound, more sound, at least, than the heartsick limb she'd gone out on. It's a wreck. Firewood. Soon to be ashes.

Never again, she thinks. You two be quiet now, she tells those headstrong sisters. Give me a break.

She tries to pull herself together by thinking ahead: to greeting her guests in the black dress with the come-to-think-of-it too puffy sleeves. Oh well. There will be the salesgirls' giggles and their sporty boyfriends. The downcast, rich brown eyes of the seamstress, an Algerian, who will let Joan know about the quality of the cous-cous without saying a word. There will be Ella singing about how she can't remember where or when. And Molly falling in love with the Frenchman, not going anywhere just yet. Joan will open all the doors, turn on all the lights.

Ernest gets an idea in his head, one of those that seems to come in a bubble. A message from afar, from obscure well-wishers. If he can help Joan to keep this Molly, then Joan will calm down, just tend her little store, stay the same old Joan. That's the ticket. He nods at himself in the mirror behind the bar. "Cheers," he says. He raises his glass and drinks. He will host the damn party alongside his loyal wife, that's what he'll do. He adjusts the patch over his eye and eats one more piece of cheese before he returns to the living room.

Joan is up on the ladder, decorating the tree.

She is round in her robe, Ernest thinks. An armful. My woman.

He hands her one of the drinks.

Joan takes it and reaches in for an ice cube. She rubs it over her face and neck. She would like to lie down, but there is still a lot to do before the guests arrive. She sips her drink and hands it back to Ernest. They look at each other, a look that lasts almost too long.

She says, "I didn't mean to—"

"Forget it."

"Okay."

Ernest says, "Merry Christmas."

Joan leans into the smell of the tree and sees the daughter that she did not have, who would have been about ten tonight, tall for her age but graceful, perhaps shy, making her way with visible reluctance across the slippery bridge between young girl and young woman. She would have taken some part in this tree-trimming, maybe helping, a fussbudget, an adorable know-it-all. Maybe just watching, listening, twisting a strand of hair around her finger, a silent smarty-pants who wonders what it's really like to be married, to be the mother and the father—wondering but glad that she does not know. And maybe, as she tucked that wayward strand of hair behind her daughter's pretty ear, Joan would think to tell her that she could sleep there tonight if she wanted, under the tree, with the lights on, and be somewhere else entirely.

* * *

    For years now Ernest has been making the long drive back and forth on Interstate 10, at least three times a week, sometimes more, to the L.A. office—the move to Palm Springs, leaving the home turf, had not been his idea—but he didn't mind. He liked the drive, liked being in the car.
    This wasn't about cars—he paid little attention to make or model. He didn't care about fast or fancy. He would tell the dealers that he wanted the thing to fit him like a pair of loose jeans and that he wanted tinted glass. The rest didn't matter. Being in the car meant that for three, four, sometimes even five hours he was in a safe place, protected from contact, from onlookers, from having to talk to anyone else as he went back and forth.
    He would listen to the radio, but not to the zealously personal voices that talked about politics or gardening or teenage pregnancies. He listened to a station that played only the good music, the old ballads, the stuff he grew up on—the songs about romance that told him nothing he didn't already know.
    He knew of course that things would not be the same, but he nevertheless swung by the old neighborhood on his way to work one day, not long after he received a telegram that informed him of his mother's painless, peaceful death, "at the ripe old age of seventy-four." She was already over-ripe, he thought, when she had me at twenty. He had tossed the telegram into the wastepaper basket from a distance, an over-handed, elegant arc, as if he were shooting a free throw, and he made it.
    He had no fond memories of the house he had lived in until he went to college, not a one, he told himself, and so no good reason to swing by and take a look at it after all these years (they've painted it turquoise, they've planted too many flowers, turned it into a doll's house, they must be girls who live there now, he thought, or queens) except to remind himself how much better off he was living in Palm Springs, spending so much time alone in his car, hour after hour, out of harm's way.

* * *

What'll I Do?

Ernest set out into the desert in a fit of serenity—focussed, he said to himself, in fact angelic, despite the heavy hiking boots and the sportsman's vest whose pockets were filled with bullets. He gave himself a nod of approval. He had been clearheaded enough to prepare a half canteen of bourbon and water, and to toss a windbreaker into the back seat, carelessly, as if nothing had happened. He was light as air, unmindful of the thicknesses of his body. There was no lingering tightness in his throat, no fear in his eyes left over from knowing what he might be capable of. He would be back in a few hours, he had said to his wife as she leaned over the dustpan, disregarding, sweeping up the glass that had shattered when it was thrown against the kitchen wall. Not *at* her, of course. He never went that far.

And he did not plan to go too far into empty county land when he pointed the car eastward with at least two hours of sun left. Wherever he was going, he would see his way there, register the signposts, remember precisely how to get back. He was not going to get himself lost in the desert. Lost, under any circumstances, anywhere, was a condition he could not bear. Getting lost was not going to happen. He would not use the word even if it did happen. He would turn it into something else.

He took the pistol with him in order to do some shooting. What he wanted was to kill a rattler, achieve a face-to-face showdown, put his serenity to some good use. Too bad, he thought, it was not in his power to give it a nightmare before he blows its head off. Make it afraid, make it sweat, make it know the everlasting gift it was about to receive from a deadly one-eyed man at peace with himself. He imagined its wide, patterned back, its long body lazily uncoiled upon a flat-topped boulder in the afternoon sun as if it would never die. The sucker.

But it was a yucca tree Ernest first took aim at, a twin-armed would-be saguaro, but with none of the stateliness, the thinness, the poise. Its fistsfulls of prickly leaves just a ruse, an empty threat. No match, Ernest said to himself, for a man with a machete, or a saw, or a Colt .45. He shot it dead center, blasting a ragged hole in its crooked torso, a juicy little pucker that exposed it for what it really was. It wouldn't take much of a cannon, he thought, to turn the whole damn thing to pulp.

He had not used the gun for years, not since he had taken it to a firing range for target practice, and he had done that only once, for a couple of hours, long enough to get the feel of it, to shoot so convincingly that he would not have to return and risk being taken for one of the regulars. Ernest could live without a gun, he was not like those other guys—even though they were onto something. Taking aim and not missing was as good as he hoped it would be, better.

His marriage, he had to admit, was also as good as he hoped it would be, insofar as hope had anything to do with it. He wasn't sure what it had to do with—apparently, it had to do with everything, and that was no help. He told himself, and sometimes he told Joan, that in fact he loved her. He may even have said so prior to throwing his chilly glass of beer against the kitchen wall—about which, as far as he was concerned, there was nothing more to say than an irredeemable waste of time at work, an incompetent secretary, the usual frustrations, minor things that just build up and build up until you can't take it anymore. And Joan was not the kind of woman you could come home to after a bad day and simply fuck. She was not like Carol with the grabable ass, the available tits. Women like Carol require no negotiations—there's nothing to it. But, come on, he had to admit that he did not much mind the negotiations, the ventures into tricky territory, the having to win Joan over. Most of the time, he was up to the challenge. He liked having to penetrate all that lean self-containment, to turn things around without giving anything up, without displaying any needs, any regrets.

It was understood, he assumed, that he had busted the glass because sometimes something had to get busted. This was not news. And it was not personal, he had said to his wife before he left the house, and then wished he hadn't because it came too close to suggesting that other things *were* personal. Ernest would be the first to decline any invitation to say which things those were. And Joan, he thought, to her credit, would be the second. That had to be one of the things he loved about her—that, and her staying power. She could go with the punches from the beginning, which was a defect only insofar as it occasionally seemed the superior stance—and on those occasions it was a serious defect. What he probably loved most about her was that she did not ask to be singled out, made no demands for special treatment, did not seem at all perturbed if he treated other people better. Like Vince. Like the guys he worked with. True, there was something about her acquiescence—he would not call it despair—that made him angry. But he didn't want it any other way. In any case, she seemed to know as well as he did how hard it was to be a man, and he couldn't help but love that about her, could he?

He took aim at another yucca, this one a bewildered-looking pom-pon girl with three mismatched arms—who should never have become part of the squad, who was too short, too shoddy, who carried her pom-pons as if they were heavier than mud. Ernest fired, unceremonious and accurate, the sound of the gun as natural as thunder, himself merely an agent of inevitable affliction, not responsible, motiveless. He smiled. He wished that he had been able to share such a moment with his father.

When he got back into the car and drove on, he pictured the machine in the hospital that would have produced the image of his father's death. He saw himself there, in a dark room, watching the machine, transfixed by the lit-up scrawl, like a child's drawing of hills and flatlands, hills and flatlands, hills and flatlands. And then suddenly no more hills. No range, all basin. No forest, all desert. It would have to have been all of a sudden. He would have been waiting for the all-of-a-suddenness that was the machine's implicit promise. He would have been waiting for it to happen, not expecting anything more from his father but that monotonous line across the screen. Then, there in the dark, he would have gotten the unexpected—the last words, miraculously uttered without recourse to the speaking device just seconds before the machine portrayed an unending desert. *Somethin's gotta give*, his father would have said.

There were hills in front of Ernest as he drove, the beginning of the Eagle mountain range to the south, farther away and smaller than it appeared in the desert light that was tightening its grip, moving in on him with its deceptive clarities and bluenesses, its theatrics of order. Sunset-sunrise, flatlands-hills, birth-death, fathers-sons, husbands-wives, swiftly go the years. He stepped on the gas, discomposed by the flabby way his mind was working. But the discomposure didn't last—the flabbiness was leaving him untouched. As well it should, he said to himself. He was remaining serene, focussed. He could let his mind do what it would, it couldn't hurt him. He turned north and headed toward Deadman's Lake, one of several dry lakes in the area. Bone dry for eons, but they still call them lakes. The way, he thought, with pleasure in the thought, he still calls Joan his wife.

Ernest had seen plenty of dry lakes in his time, and none of them had ever looked to him like an enormous mistake, a wound in the earth. They looked instead like lakes that just happened, for the moment, to be empty. You can't see one, he said to himself, and not see it full of water, dotted with young skiers and sullen fishermen. You know what a lake is supposed to look like and you see it even if it isn't there, even though you are looking at something that is barren and sadly unbeautiful, as though it remembered having once been beautiful, like a widow.

He imagined Joan in a weather-beaten widow's walk, seated, with her knees pulled up against her chest, waiting for someone to come along and look after her, pretending to be doing something else, pretending to need nothing but stamina and cigarettes and Ernest. It was a good thing, he thought, that she had no knowledge of the gun. Not that she would use it against him. It was unlikely that she would even touch it, more likely, in fact, that she would touch her husband's cock, which she didn't do much of, not nearly enough of, and when she did it was still the way it had always been—a little regretful, a little aggressive, a little sincere—which he had almost always managed to disregard. But the gun—she might think that he would use it against *her*, on one of his bad days, which he would never do. He would sooner use it against himself. He had kept it carefully hidden because he did not want to have to make such a declaration. It would sound false to both of them, somebody else's line, a hero's oath, even though, as far as he knew, he would mean it.

Driving with his left hand, he picked up the gun with his right and touched the muzzle to his temple. Pow, he said out loud. You're a goner. Then he laughed and put the gun down, feeling like a kid playing hooky, just taking a ride in his car, breaking the speed limit, going nowhere in particular, going anywhere but home, flirting with dangerous thoughts. He heard his father's mocking chuckle—a memory that made him, while it lasted, oddly grateful.

If he were home now he would be having a drink. So he reached for the canteen, held it between his knees while he twisted the cap off, and then took a swig worthy of a kid playing hooky, breaking the rules. He was ready for action, ready to display some unusual agility, to be light on his feet, gunman and acrobat, the Jack of Spades. He eased up on the gas and turned onto an unmarked dirt road that seemed bound to contain a snake or two, slow-moving targets, inching their way from one side to the other, like blind pedestrians that try a man's patience and deserve to be shot.

The things that tried a man's patience—the list could go on forever, Ernest said to himself. Starting with all manner of equipment and machinery and gadgets. Then office parties, holidays, anniversaries of births and deaths and marriages. All secretaries and most waitresses. Grown men and women who kissed in public. *Being* in public. Standing in lines. Being talked to by strangers, especially by women, especially if his wife were in the vicinity, because she would know that he was being called upon to be patient and polite and that he wanted to be neither, so that he would have to force himself goddamnit to be patient and polite in order to prove that his wife was mistaken, that he was full of surprises, that he could perform with the best of them, unrehearsed.

The road itself turned out to be lifeless, empty of even so much as a rustle, but it led him to what he needed. He pulled over, stopped the car, and put on his windbreaker. About two hundred yards away a lengthy, gorgeous arrangement of boulders was offering itself as a perfect hide-out for snakes. He would go there, just close enough to take some shots and frighten a big one into view. Then the show-down: he would not allow the threatening rattle to undo him. He would win this one, achieve a clean kill to the head, take the thing home to his wife. He would celebrate, make her forget about the earlier scene. And he would have a belt made from the skin, two of them if possible—his and hers. He took another long drink from the canteen and reloaded the empty cylinders, shaking off a sudden heaviness, a chill, a wishing that he were not alone. As he headed for the mound of boulders, he stuck the gun in the waistband of his jeans and gave it a pat. Again he heard his father's wry laughter—which was a comfort, of a sort. Sure it was, Ernest told himself.

He stood still for a moment and took in the stunning rock formation. It looked to him like a wide-hipped, big-breasted woman lying on her side, facing him, as if she were waiting, as if the desert floor were a silken couch. She was all indolence and milkiness, content, even saucy in her extravagant womanhood—heaps of naked flesh glittering with mica and quartz. Huge, chalky, sand-colored breasts, a cleavage into which a man could vanish. Solid plumpnesses everywhere that defied thought, that were meant only to be stroked and turned into refuge, climbed onto and into, easily, easily conquered. She was waiting, nearly swooning, hot and pink and voluptuous. He imagined one of her hands, as in a painting he had seen once, gently touching her pubic hair—the hand there, not so much demurely obscuring as calling attention to her sex, to his, to theirs, asking for it, saying come and get it, get it and come, big boy.

The guys he did field work with—they should be here, he thought. They would love this dame. They would carry on about her abundant attributes. And Ernest would tell them about the painting, the hand—which would lead to a mad gathering of tumbleweeds, a scrambling up onto the boulders, harrowing leaps, and the creation of a pubic bush of awesome proportions. Then they would stand back for a good view of their handiwork, bump elbows, laugh, it would be great. Somebody else should be here, he thought. It would not be the same with Joan as it would be with the guys—but it would be better than nothing. He could do all the carrying on, taunt her with it, pull a remark out of her that would make the taunting worth it.

By himself, the boulder dame was not much fun to think about. He went toward her, staring at his feet as he walked, mulling over the options—he could go back to the car and keep driving, he could do anything he wanted, he could fire all six rounds into her if he wanted, the cunt. Forget it, he told himself. He was not going to let anything clog him up. He reached for his gun, hefted it. He was fine, he thought. He would do what he set out to do, and he would bring home a trophy, turn things around. He was a man with a mission, light as air.

As he approached the luxurious mound of boulders—more red than pink now, he thought, drenched in shadow and receding sunlight, but nothing he wanted to enter, merely a snake-pit—he was so focussed that he almost didn't see the bones, almost stepped right on top of the stark remnants of what at first appeared to have been a child or a youth, an innocent curled up against a solitary and indifferent rock. For a moment Ernest was not sure whether it was real, whether he was seeing things, whether he was imagining it the way he had imagined the come-and-get-it woman. But it was real all right. And it seemed to have been hugging the rock in its death, clinging and clutching as if the rock might take it as its own, protect and keep it. What was left of the teeth indicated an adult—but the rest told a story of an adult small enough to have been an easy target for whatever rage it was that had turned itself into hacking and smashing, all those broken bones, a shattered skull. Ernest took a closer look. Wedged beneath the rock was a piece of leather belt, branded with the name "Roy."

It was an unseemly death, and it was making demands that Ernest did not want to hear, but couldn't keep himself from hearing—pitiful, grotesque demands that he *do* something, please, help it to disappear, not be exposed like that, clutching and clinging, horribly fetal, subject to comment and conjecture from strangers, who would no doubt comment on what a small man he had been, not much over five feet (a small man with a kingly name, bad combination from the start, they would say), and how it was probably, surely the case that he had been a belligerent smart-ass to make up for what he lacked in body (they would speak of the thin, girlish arms and legs, the delicate hands; they would presume a wee dick but would not mention it out of respect for the dead), and how he must have picked a fight, that Roy, asked for it and got it in spades, got himself definitively killed (every bone in his body, would you look at that?), and how sweetly childlike he had become at the end (they would say that he must have looked like an angel as a child, made his mother so proud). One humiliating remark after another. *Do something*, the thing seemed to be saying. I would do it for you. We have to stick together. I wouldn't let any strangers find you like this, all broken and unmanned, I swear I wouldn't.

A likely story, Ernest said to himself as he sat down beside the ashy bones and opened the canteen. The evening breeze blew humps and bulges into his lightweight jacket, and he imagined how he must look—hunchbacked and crazy, half-blind, thickly over-the-hill. He felt like leering, like shouting something incomprehensible and threatening, like playing the madman. And so he did. He produced a slack-mouthed snarling wail that echoed among the placid boulders, and then another, louder still, a deeply satisfying nightmarish roar.

He looked at the bones, reached over and touched a splintered femur, and told himself that he was sitting in the sandy dirt in the middle of nowhere next to this man's remains because he was tired, because he had had a rough day, because it was hard to be somebody's husband, somebody's son, somebody's friend.

He almost felt sorry for Roy. He did not know what to do. He was half-way inclined to look after the goddamn corpse. He wished that Joan were there. But he would not, later, let himself say so. He would get over it, this whatever it was, that was making his body sag, making his feet go limp, so that the tips of his boots pointed in opposite, clownish directions. One thing he could say about Joan: she wouldn't laugh at him, if she saw him like this, he was sure of it. She wouldn't ask for explanations. She would leave him alone, but he wouldn't be by himself, sagging as if all the air had left his body. She would let him sag, and she would keep the stray onlooker away from him, protect him from gossip and speculation. She would let him do what he would—howl like a fool, shoot off his gun, shoot off his mouth, sit slumped in the dirt not knowing what to do—without taking any of it personally. She would look out for him, of course she would, there was no one else. And she would cover you up, Roy. You can bet on it.

But why take any chances, Ernest asked himself. What if she did, in fact, in that private way of hers, take any of it personally? What if she believed that he wanted her to leave him alone? Simple, he told himself. He would make some changes, some adjustments, he could do that without losing any ground, without having to come right out and say that he did not want to end up all by himself, like some lost kid who wants his mommy. Like you, Roy.

Ernest got himself up, thinking that some other time, soon, when he was not so weary, he would hunt down a major snake, have the belts made, or at least one of them, the one for his wife. He would surprise her with it, with his courage and thoughtfulness—he imagined the pleased look on her face, his offering to thread it through her belt-loops, her edgy acquiescence. It played well, that scene. They would be all right. They'd been all right for all this time, hadn't they? Ernest headed for the car, unburdened, re-focussed, not listening to the low laughter that was at his back as the sun went down.

* * *

There is a mountain there, Mt. San Jacinto, that presides over the desert city. It seems to Joan to have been removed from its place of birth and repositioned in order to keep the leather-skinned desert-dwellers uneasy, to keep them thinking about how it is up there, at the top, on any given day, in the cool, leafy forest. It is simple enough, on any given day, to find out—by driving around to the western side and taking the road up to Idyllwild, or by taking the tram that eases its way up through a rocky corridor on the Palm Springs side.

Joan had never been up there. The mountain seemed to her to be an intrusive heap of dreamland, almost bullying, too beckoning, too promising. It haunted the desert with its exaggerated impression of difference—its craggy, looming face, spruced up with sprays of wildflowers, always implying that a change of scene, of scent, of light might change her life.

When she was as certain as she could be that it was far too late for that, she finally boarded the tram one summer evening after work. There was one other passenger, a young, perhaps thirty-five-year-old man who looked at her only once, and whose eyes seemed wedded, in sickness and in health, to panic. "I go up once a week," he said. She needed to ignore the panic, there was too little she could do for him, she knew too little of solace, so she asked what it was like up there, in the forest, at the top of the mountain. "I don't know," he told her. "I come right back down." She assumed that he liked the ride in the tram, the lifting, the floating, that it soothed him, dispelled the fear, at least for a while. But she was wrong. "Call it Russian roulette," he explained, not looking at her, not looking at anything. "I'm certain each and every time that the cable will break. I'm positive."

This possibility had not occurred to her—but now that it did, she thought that such an end to her having capitulated to the dreamy seduction of the mountain would be fitting. She thought that she wouldn't mind much, hardly at all, and she hoped that the roulette player wouldn't either, that he wouldn't scream, wouldn't clutch at her, would let the thing just take them and tumble.

She looked out the windows, allowed the tram to offer its grand view as it carried her up and up, allowed herself to imagine not a break in the cable but an extension—so that the tram would keep going, float skyward, beyond the top of the mountain, beyond the cozy, reassuring odors of the forest, beyond the lasting, hand-in-hand trees, to whatever might be out there, out of reach.

* * *

But Not for Me

"Things kept in memory of, or on behalf of the giver."

Joan re-read these words and wondered where in the dictionary she might find the right name for the things she had kept. It seemed important that she be precise. She was thinking: precision as safety net, as life-jacket. And "keepsakes" wouldn't do, according to this definition, since her things were not given, none of them had passed from someone else's hands to her own. The postcards from Molly and from Charles were a kind of exception—but neither of them would attach to their brief missives the weight of a keepsake.

The sticking-point of the giver, she supposed, could be ignored. The things could be kept for their own sakes, couldn't they? Joan flipped again through the pages of the dictionary and reminded herself that this would mean keeping them for their own good, for their safety or benefit. And this, too, would not do. Were she to measure the little good she had enacted by keeping these things in the filing cabinet at her dress shop, she would come up with nothing. With pointless, inconsequential hanging-on: she sees herself as would-be sailor who harbors only a shipwreck, who tucks into a tidy dock the scraps of a boat she might once have boarded but never did—never said to herself, I'll set sail, come what may.

Laid out before her on the desk in her office, Joan's collection of fragments spoke without eloquence of inadequately-begun and never-quite-ended stories. Their voices reminded her of the way a shy girl announces her name in a public forum: she is reluctant to suggest that her name is vital, that it matters, that it ought to be noted, so she says it and swallows it at the same time.

There was another possibility—but she could not, truthfully, claim that she had kept these things for her own sake. She did not need them in order to remember, for she remembered all too well, without ever, or almost ever, opening the drawer for a look, a touch. Neither did they provide a sense of continuity and togetherness. They did not add up to a richly-textured history in which relations both distant and close swirl about each other, for better or worse, in some wonderful dance, connected forever as if by magnetic force, moving together toward recompense if not resolution, toward inklings if not enlightenment.

It was dawn and Joan was alone in her shop. She still had plenty of time to make the long drive to Balboa Island. She could stall a while longer over terminology, to tell herself some words that fit, that named the things she would no longer keep, that introduced them to one another, and might turn them into a kind of family, the kind that dies far too soon or otherwise disperses.

Everything else was ready: she had used the pants as a winding-sheet in which to wrap the other items, then secured the bundle with heavy string. She had dismantled the photograph of her parents and distributed the weight of the glass and the frame. The bundle was well-balanced, tight and neat, v-shaped. She knew, or thought she knew, what an item was, but she looked it up anyway, gave herself a few more minutes of hesitation. And she ended up giving herself the unsettling redundancy of "a separate particular," the familiar, too appropriate "piece of news," and something else, designated obsolete, but wasn't that at all—"a warning, a hint."

Item: Size 8 cotton pants, white, with pockets in the back but not the front; wrinkled as if they had been bunched up and used as a pillow, then hugged and dreamt upon. The pants are stained near the cuff of the right leg with something pungent and insistent, that won't let go, like sap, like Vince.

Item: A man's Timex wristwatch, retrieved from the trashcan in the bedroom. It is extra-wide, gold-plated, with black roman numerals on a white face. Etched on the back is an inscription, vintage Jerry, a message to his son, a quotation from Groucho Marx: "Time wounds all heels."

Item: One color photograph, 5 x 7, framed in austere Danish sterling, with a green velvet backing. The frame cost the purchaser, then twelve years old, six months' worth of allowance. At the time, she placed the photograph on the chest of drawers, where she could see it, see them, from anyplace else in her bedroom; later, when she lived in an apartment, she placed it on the mantle over the fireplace. There are two people in the photograph, William and Elena. The man is handsome, about six feet tall, and slender. His hair is light brown and combed straight back from his forehead. He has large gray eyes and a mouth that young girls would describe as kissable, except that in the photograph there is a tightness at the corners of his kissable mouth. His body, which is turned toward the woman in the photograph, seems to be separate from his head, which is facing the camera; he is looking over his shoulder and almost smiling. The woman in the photograph is five-and-a-half feet tall. Her shoulder-length hair is dark brown and wavy; her eyes are almond-shaped and almost black. People of all ages would describe her face as beautiful. Her petite, perfectly proportioned body is facing the camera, one hip arched up against the man she is standing next to. But her beautiful smiling face is looking the other way, away from him, toward someone who is not part of the picture.

Item: A newspaper clipping from the *Los Angeles Times*; two half-page columns plus photo. The headline reads: "Wrong Man Slain." The story describes the wrong man as a long-time resident of the Beverly Hills Hotel, "no trouble whatsoever," who had no known relatives. It goes on to explain that several witnesses saw him grabbed from behind, saw his assailant cut his throat, saw the assailant kick the dead body. The assailant did not attempt to avoid capture. On the contrary, he wanted his crime to be witnessed: he had telephoned his girlfriend and asked her to meet him in the hotel parking lot, with the intention of displaying to her the dead body of her lover. When he learned from her that he had killed the wrong man, he seemed bewildered at first, then said it didn't matter, he was satisfied. Perhaps this is why the two policemen in the photo are smiling; perhaps they think that the assailant is funny; perhaps they think that a man with no known relatives doesn't matter very much. The slain man, the wrong man, is covered with a beach towel, but not fully covered: his feet are visible, and they do not look dead. They look like feet that would prefer dancing to just about anything else. One hand is also visible, the left one: the palm is up and open, but it does indeed look dead, not like a hand that one could pick up and press against one's face and body.

Item: A postcard—the only one—from Molly, who did fall in love with the French sportswear manufacturer, and who not only quit her job but quit without notice. And so did he. Two days after Joan's Christmas party, they were on their way to his place in Barcelona. On the front of the postcard is a black-and-white photograph of a downed matador, lying on his back. His knees are bent back toward his chest and his feet are raised as if they might protect him from the leaping bull whose front hooves are about to land on him. The postcard reads: "Sorry to leave in such a rush. But these last-chance-times are hard to come by, and I am aiming for hundreds of them. Do the same, boss."

Item: Another postcard—one of many from the sender, but the only one that Joan has saved. The color photo depicts an aerial view of the island of Moorea, which can be seen from Tahiti. Moorea has been home to the courtly Charles since shortly after the death of his friend and roommate, Jerry. On the back, Charles writes: "My dear child, they tell me that it is at last my turn. I will put myself and my piano aboard an outrigger and die singing to the mermaids in these brilliant waters. It will be grand, I assure you, my dear girl."

Joan lingered for a moment over this item. Charles's correspondence always included some reference to Joan as his child, his girl. It was as if the hundreds of miles of ocean that had long since separated them made another, even dearer relation possible. When his postcards began to arrive, Joan at first accepted, and then embraced, and came to treasure that "my dear child" since she did not have to worry, did not have to pray for some means to keep the tender owner of the phrase from going away, as all the others did. He was already gone, easy to love.

It was ten o'clock, an exceptionally foggy morning, when Joan boarded the mid-sized motor boat she had hired for the day. The boat belonged to a man named Henry, who took out-of-town fishermen or small groups of partiers out to the deep ocean waters and then, after the fish had been caught or the beer drunk, brought them back delighted and sunburned.

He took Joan's hand as she stepped into the boat and asked when the others would arrive. Then he apologized for having to charge her the usual minimum-four-person amount when she told him that there would be no others, that she was alone. He was gentlemanly, deeply tanned, round in face and body, like a gingerbread man, and, she guessed, about sixty years old. He showed her the narrow cabin, pointed to what he called the ladies' room, and explained that the bow was off limits, too risky. She could set herself down anyplace else, there were sandwiches and coffee in the locker on the starboard side.

Joan took a seat near the back of the boat, and regarded the easy pride with which her captain handled his boat. She was more than relieved at her luck. She could tell that she had picked the right name from the list provided by one of her regular customers who lived in Newport but golfed in Palm Springs. This Henry was clearly not a blowhard, not a seafaring cowboy who would talk too much and want to carouse—though it was not Henry's name that drew her, it was the name of his boat: *S'Wonderful*.

"Harbor tour?" he asked. "Or are we heading out?"

"We're heading out."

"Suits me," he said. "Can't see much of anything in particular this morning."

The fog horns bellowed their warnings as the boat in low gear glided past the dangerously invisible jetty. The water was a dark gray, impervious, smooth and waveless until they left the bay behind. Even the undulating ocean seemed to Joan subdued, preoccupied with the heavy fog, with the orange and yellow lights that flashed as if attached to nothing from the few boats daring enough to have entered that gray dream. There was no view of the long Newport peninsula, the piers, the houses crowded along the beachfront—there was nothing but fog. The boat seemed to have left everything familiar behind, to have passed through into some other state of affairs, in which there are no states of affairs, only states of moisture, dense water below, filmy water above, silent and insinuating bedfellows.

"I *love* this!" Henry called out. He did not turn to look at his passenger, asked for no response. He seemed to have made his declaration simply because it had to be made, because it was true.

Reason enough, Joan thought. And not dissimilar to the reason, such as it was, that she was on board, clutching her tightly-bound bundle of items—she was doing this because it had to be done. Because her items seemed to have been asking something from her that she had not given, asking for a while now, and her refusals had resulted only in more vivid memories and more frequent naps.

She had no expectations. She was not willing to believe that she was driven by any notion that what she would do would make a difference, would mark a distinction between this day and the days to come, would signal something like renewal, like hope. If she had to say what had finally pushed her, implanted the idea, told her to empty the drawer in her filing cabinet, then she would keep it simple: she would say that it was age, that it was fatigue. And she would see no good reason to spell it out.

She would not give in to saying that she was tired to the point of wanting nothing but sleep from the strenuous work of keeping herself from naming things she did not want to name. She was tired even though she had not done this work alone. After all, she thought, for more than twenty years she had been assisted by her husband, her co-conspirator, so to speak, who was even more adept than she was at keeping things at bay.

Her husband: as in a magus at the arts of detachment and cautious desire. A man who would sooner impersonate himself than let things get too personal. He was apparently untouchable, a perfect mate. Almost. Not easy to love, though neither, she knew, was she—but expressions of that order were precisely what together they worked on keeping out of the picture. They worked on it with the same quiet ardor that others might work on taking care of each other, on saying what had to be said before it was too late.

Best, she thought, to give up on the lurking matter of her husband, on what they had done for and with and to each other. Best not to wonder what relinquishing her items and their unspoken, incessant demands would portend for a marriage kept afloat by its undercurrents. She supposed that she and her husband would continue as they always had.

Joan found herself holding the bundle in the crook of her arm as if it were an infant, and she found herself not correcting that snug embrace, letting it happen, letting herself take a good look at what else she had been hanging onto, the gift she had not accepted, and for which there was no remnant, nothing to have kept in the drawer. There was nothing but an imagined face, a little-girl version of the beautiful young woman in that room in Ensenada who had said *Sí, bueno.*

And in that face there was everything that Joan had from early on hoped to evade—as if, to do otherwise, she would bring upon herself the fear of those whose hair turns white, whose mouths remain forever agape in a petrified scream. In the imagined face of her unborn child was its need to be kept from harm, a need impossible to meet, to even contemplate.

Harm wins, hands down, every time: that Joan could contemplate, that she could live up to, that she was certain of. She cradled her items, the irrefutable proof, in her arms.

There was only the sound of the motor, a lion's purring, and the soft splash of the underbelly of the hull as the boat lifted and dipped, lifted and dipped over the subdued, dark swells. The breeze was strong, but not strong enough to turn itself into a wind, and it seemed to Joan to be mingling with the fog, moseying, not at all inclined to herd the fog back somewhere and out of the way. She got up and stood for a while beneath the awning, next to Henry.

The two of them looked out over the rhythmic up-and-down of the bow at the dense, endless cloud they had entered.

"Coffee?" he asked.

"Not yet, thanks."

Henry looked at her and at the bundle she was holding. But he didn't ask. She would have to tell him.

"Do people hire out your boat for burials at sea?"

"Not so far." He looked again, but not for long.

She saw the way his rough hands appreciated the glossy mahogany of the wheel, and she wondered how he lived, what his home was like, whether there were daily, intimate recipients of his gentle reticence, his ability to say *I love this!* She wondered whether his amiable blue eyes looked upon anyone first thing in the morning.

"I'll leave it up to you," she said, "when to stop the boat." She returned then to her seat at the back.

"I'll pick a good spot!" Henry called out.

And he did. After another half an hour he turned off the motor in a spot that looked no different from any other spot within the fog-cloud, but because he had picked it, it seemed to Joan distinctly good.

Henry did not leave his seat at the helm, nor did he turn around in order to observe his passenger's next move. He draped his flannel-covered arms over the wide wooden wheel and stared straight ahead, waiting—so that, Joan thought, if she wanted to, if it were part of the plan, she could tuck the bundle underneath her thick blue sweater and then ease herself over, into the water, quietly, unheeded, as if she'd never been there in the first place, thankful for the ultimate privacy. And she was thankful in any case. She had not looked forward to the prospect of being witnessed as she discarded the belongings that she had not, until now, let belong to her, nor she to them.

Joan stood and faced the water. She was unsteady at first—almost faint with the burden of her incompletions, the stories that might have been within her reach, and the letting go that was. But she gave herself over to the tilting of the boat, to being rocked by a gray and dreary ocean that asked nothing in return, no gratitude, no blessing. Joan hugged the bundle and let herself be rocked.

Later, she would not know how long she stood there and finally grieved for her dead, her parents, her lost friends, a man she loved. She would not remember the point at which her regrets became an incoherent blur, indistinguishable from her desire to put them to rest. But she would remember that she did not resist, did not put up any fight against knowing what her grief felt like—and that she had nonetheless remained standing. And she would remember the moment when she held the bundle in one hand, away from her and back, as she had seen baseball pitchers do, just before she swung her package into the fog. She would remember crying out, *"I love you!"*

But it was a bad toss.

Something—her blind, inexpert throw, or perhaps the boomerang shape of the bundle, or perhaps the laughing mean-spiritedness of the sea gods—whatever it was, something made her tightly-packed items sail in a curve right back into the boat.

It crashed against the base of the captain's chair and so startled Henry that he thrust one knee up against the wheel and splashed his coffee all over the white pants. He would have picked it up, immediately, the thing at his feet, to wipe it off, to try some fruitless salvaging with hot water or with salt, but he stopped himself lest his touching it commit some further profanation.

He turned to look at Joan, who was looking at him. The two of them were frozen in wonderment, each mirroring the other's confused posture, the open-handed appeal: his eyes were asking what had happened, what he could do to help; her eyes were streaked with helpless anguish, hovering above the empty space between disbelief and dismay.

"Is it relics?" Henry asked.

Joan was speechless. She nodded and reached out a hand—a lunatic hand, it seemed to her, unattached, claw-like, gesturing toward the bundle, or perhaps toward Henry, in order to get hold of something, someone, there being, this time, no question of her getting hold of herself.

Henry went to her, and took up the wavering hand. He patted and politely stroked her shoulder, giving what he could, waiting for her to speak. He waited a long time.

"It came back," she finally whispered. "It all came back."

"Yes, well—"

"I needed, I mean, I meant to let them—" Her free hand, fish-like and swiftly swimming, made a gesture that completed the sentence.

"Could it be, missus, that you are meant to hang on?"

"I don't know. I don't think so." Joan looked at him again. "No," she said. "I'm to do this."

"My guess is, then, you must have thrown it right into the wind. That's all."

Joan looked into Henry's considerate, appeasing face. "I don't have to keep them."

"Not unless you have a rule against second chances."

This caught her up, pulled her forward with a yank. "I do," she told him.

"Well then."

The silence, this time, was awkward. Joan did not let it last for long.

"I'd like to break that rule."

"May I recommend an easy drop straight off the stern?"

"You may." She watched as he turned back toward the cabin.

Henry picked up the disheveled bundle as if it were a genuine relic and brought it to her. He remained at her side, but looked the other way as she held her items one last time. When she finally leaned forward, she felt a steadying hand on her elbow. Together, they watched the bundle float for a moment, then disappear.

Something was over. Joan was not sure what.

Henry was still looking out at the ocean swells when he asked, "Shall we head back?"

Anywhere but back, Joan said to herself. But to Henry she said, "Yes. And thank you."

"May I recommend a sandwich and a cup of coffee?"

"You may."

Henry looked at Joan and smiled. "Rest assured, missus, I know what I'm doing when it comes to food and drink."

Over a lunch of curried tuna sandwiches on fresh sourdough bread, they exchanged some small talk, about the boat, about her dress shop. Then Henry started the engine and turned the boat toward the coastline they could not see. But it was easy enough for Joan to see what otherwise lay ahead: she knew what the drive down to Palm Springs would be like, the speedings-up and the slowings-down, the crowded isolation, the unnerving smell of the traffic, the smog, the starkness that awaited her once she reached the desert highway, the sharp edges that awaited her at home. For now, she moved to the seat next to Henry, beneath the awning, as they headed back through the lifting fog.

* * *

There will be no suicides in this story, no crimes of passion. In which case, we are left to imagine them, Joan and Ernest, moving together, stride for stride, into old age.

But we don't want to imagine this. We don't like what we see when we imagine this. Not at all.

So we'll imagine instead that these two do manage to throw in the towel while they are still, but barely, in their fifties, and that it is an amicable split. We won't let them be resentful and petty. They'll keep in touch, not frequently but genially—the way grown-up brothers and sisters do, who become much happier with each other once they no longer have to share a bathroom, much less the attention of their distracted parents.

We can sell the dress shop in Palm Springs and send Joan to Barcelona, where she will spend a month with Molly and the Frenchman, recoup one of her losses, before she heads off on her own to, say, Tuscany. There, let's give her a memorable evening in San Gimignano—you fill in the blanks, as you wish.

And let's say that, afterwards, she decides to settle in Rome for a while. She has discovered that the language of the natives comes naturally to her—who would have thought? Not Joan, that's certain. But it's true—which makes it all the more difficult for us to see her as just another idle American tourist. So we'll give her a job as a consultant for an Italian fashion designer, who can't get over how good she is.

When last we see her, it is summertime in Rome. She is sitting alone in a semi-swank cafe, in her oversized sunglasses and a billowy white dress. There is a summer flower of some sort tucked above her right ear. She is reading a note from her ex-husband.

Joan would have wanted Ernest to have the house in Palm Springs, so we'll go along with it—whether or not we approve of the bachelor parties he held there after she departed. Pornographic movies and the like. But we'll be kind.

Let's be kind enough to bring to Ernest's house, on a night when there is no party, his co-worker Howard (Lola—we're not surprised—did not, after all, fit the bill, or wouldn't pay). And let's say that, within no time, Howard becomes Ernest's roommate. Howard's pet name for Ernest is Cyclops. Ernest calls his roommate Howie or sometimes Howdy-Doody. We'll imagine that they laugh a lot. After all, they can do whatever they want, out in the open. And they do.

We'll assume that Howard does all the cooking, and that he has put Ernest on a diet. They go for a two-mile jog just about every morning. Howard is trying to quit smoking. Ernest is not trying to give up his martinis; nevertheless, let's imagine that he feels a whole lot better.

We'll give ourselves a last glimpse of him in the deep end of the swimming pool. He is underwater, holding his breath, and thinking about the note he intends to send to Joan. It's been a while since he's written. One thing he knows for sure: he wants to begin with a line from one of the old songs. *I could cry salty tears, where have I been all these years?*

About the Author

Melissa Malouf grew up and was educated in Southern California. For the last many years, she has been teaching literature and creative writing at Duke University, where she is an award-winning professor. She has been a Breadloaf Fellow and is a regular book reviewer for the N.C. *News&Observer*. One of the stories in her first book, *No Guarantees*, was awarded the Pushcart Prize.

0-595-32324-3

Printed in the United States
20472LVS00006B/508-579